ISLAND QUARRY

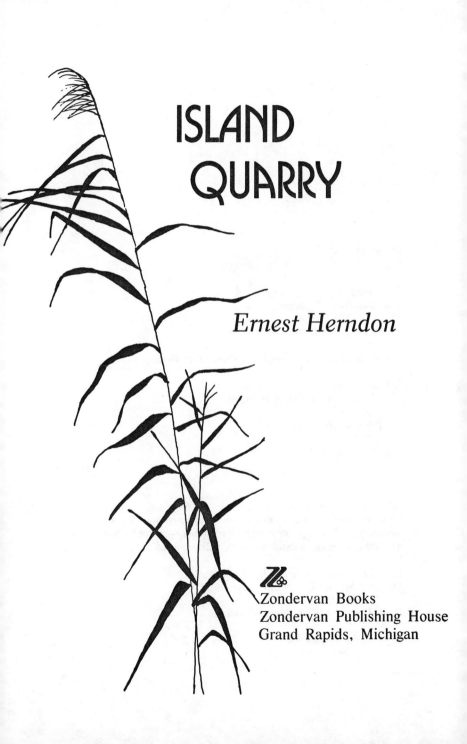

ISLAND QUARRY

Ernest Herndon

Zondervan Books
Zondervan Publishing House
Grand Rapids, Michigan

ISLAND QUARRY
Copyright © 1990 by Ernest Herndon

Zondervan Books is an imprint of
The Zondervan Publishing House
1415 Lake Drive, S.E.
Grand Rapids, Michigan 49506

Library of Congress Cataloging-in-Publication Data:

Herndon, Ernest.
    Island quarry / Ernest Herndon.
        p.   cm.
    ISBN 0-310-27581-4
    I. Title
PS3558.E689I8   1990
813'.54—dc20   90–33801
                                                                CIP

Edited by Joyce Ellis and Lori Walburg
Designed by Ann Cherryman

Printed in the United States of America

90 91 92 93 94 95 / AK / 10 9 8 7 6 5 4 3 2 1

● ● ●

To Tom Seabourne,
Nancy Knightly-Vogel,
and Joe Cannon, Jr.
And with endless thanks
to my wife Angelyn Herndon.

● ● ●

It is at times as though the eyes burned hard and glad
And did not take the goat path quivering to the right,
Wide of the mountain—thence to tears and sleep—
But went on into marble that does not weep.

Hart Crane
"Island Quarry"

CHAPTER 1

● ● ●

He walked out of the chilly airport into the muggy predawn air of Guam, a small flight bag hanging from his shoulder, suitcases in both hands. In the semidarkness he could see the silhouettes of rooftops and beyond them the colorless slate of the sea. It felt good to be on an island again.

He did not immediately hail a taxi—they were lined up in front of the airport, the drivers mostly sleeping—but instead sat down on a concrete bench beside a fragrant tropical bush. His body lost in jet lag, his mind buoyant in realms of fatigue, he packed his meerschaum with tobacco, and soon the Danish vanilla aroma surrounded him. He leaned back, weary from twenty-odd hours in transit, and relaxed, watching the sky slowly pale.

The tropical dawn assumed its colors like a dark woman wrapping herself in a sarong perfumed with vanilla, raintree, and Pacific Ocean. The sky over a big rocky cliff to his right began to glow with brassy light. The sea before him lit up as though touched by a wand, staining it pink. Rooftops glimmered. The air seemed to crackle with coming day.

Carl Connolly tapped the crust of ashes out of his pipe and relit it. Smoke blossomed, then was whisked away by a light breeze. When he finished smoking, he felt hot under the rising sun and very tired, no longer able to savor the morning. He walked to a cab and mentioned the name of his hotel. The driver named a price, which Carl knew was too high, but he got in.

At the hotel a Japanese clerk checked him in and gave him a key. Carl walked outside and down the sidewalk among small palm trees to his ground-level room. Before he unlocked the door, he glanced down the walk to the beach. After he had rested it would be good to go to the beach for the afternoon and drink a cold beer and swim and sunbathe and read.

Entering his room, Carl Connolly's shoulders sagged with mild disappointment. The accommodations certainly were not fine enough to merit the price he had paid. Nor, despite the humming air conditioner, was it cool. Laying his luggage on one bed, he removed his shoes and socks, trudged into the bathroom to wash his face and hands, then stretched out on the other bed.

Later, rested but not having slept, he phoned the airline that had his connecting flight. A small company, its desk had been closed when he arrived that morning. It should be open now.

A woman came on the line, and he told her he would like to confirm his flight to Okinawa the next morning.

She seemed confused. "There is no flight to Okinawa from here."

Her words jolted him. He sat up and opened his ticket envelope. "But I have a ticket here on your airline. It says a flight leaves at 7:30 in the morning for Okinawa."

"Sir, that flight has not run since October."

"I have the ticket in my hand."

"Let me have you talk to the manager."

A man's voice sounded in Carl's ear. "May I help you?"

Carl repeated his story.

"Who sold you that ticket?"

"I bought it from a travel agent in New Orleans."

"Well, he sold you a worthless ticket."

"But he confirmed it with your airline. I was there when he did it."

"I'm sorry, sir. There is no flight from Guam to Okinawa."

"Do you mean to tell me that I have a ticket here on your airline that I paid money for, and you're saying it's no good?"

"I'm sorry, sir. We'll do whatever we can to reroute you."

"What about the money?"

"I'm afraid there's nothing we can do about that here. You'll have to get in touch with your travel agent about that."

Carl gripped the receiver with a sweaty hand. "So how do I get to Okinawa?"

"Just a minute."

Canned South Sea island music came over the line. Carl felt nauseated. The man returned.

"We can route you either through the Philippines or Tokyo."

"Which flight leaves sooner?"

"The one to Manila leaves at six tomorrow morning. To Tokyo, eight tomorrow evening. The price is roughly the same, and both have an overnight layover."

"Book me on the Manila flight."

When he had negotiated the details, he lay back on his bed. His heart was throbbing, and the room seemed to whirl about him. He had not slept in twenty-four hours, and now sleep was out of the question. He went into the bathroom to take a shower.

Later, as he sat in a cushioned wrought-iron chair, shaded by a table umbrella and drinking cold beer, things did not seem as bad. The air was hot but the breeze felt good. Maybe he had overreacted, being so tired. Maybe it was all a harmless mistake, an accidental booking on a discontinued flight.

The beach and the sea were dazzling. Emerald cliffs ranged around the bay. The water was brush-stroked with the bright colors of windsurfers' sails. Pale GIs sunbathed on the sand, heedless of the agonies they were inflicting on their skin. Honeymooning Japanese couples sat together on beach towels. Clusters of young Americans sat at other tables. A radio played rock music, lively and loud.

Carl ordered a cheeseburger and another beer. Opening his detective novel, he read desultorily. He had checked out everyone around him, casually. No one looked suspicious. Soothed, he ate the burger and delved into the novel.

That night he slept well but woke for no reason at four in the morning. Wide awake, he decided to go for a stroll on the beach.

Outside, the tropical night was pure, scented heaven—balmy, cool, with a breeze off the sleepy sea. Not a person stirred. He passed the outdoor café where he had eaten earlier and stood in the sand, listening to the murmur of the water.

Suddenly he became possessed by the certainty that someone was watching him. He scanned his surroundings. A few lights twinkled down the beach. Behind him, the motel's outdoor sodium lights threw eerie shadows.

He looked back to the ocean, and his breath caught suddenly. Was that someone out there, standing in the water?

He backed up slowly, squinting to see more clearly. It made no sense at all—yet he could almost see someone, motionless in the shallow water many yards out, watching patiently. Carl's skin prickled the length of his body.

Turning, he hurried back to his room. Inside, he locked and chained the door, his heart pounding.

Carl stretched out on his bed, afraid to turn the lights

out. Passing a palm across his sweat-damp forehead, he tried to sleep.

● ● ●

On the flight to Manila Carl felt jumpy, his insides queasy. He tried to eat the food served him, hoping it would settle his stomach, but his long diet of airplane food was getting to him. He found it repulsive. Leaving the food alone, he drank black coffee. The coffee in this part of the world was good, anyway.

Below him, at last, he saw the bold, jungle-massed mountains and huge swampy brown lakes of the Philippines. Later the murky slums of Manila appeared beneath him. He had never been to the Philippines before and felt none too good about these circumstances. He kept expecting trouble anytime. The man could be on this plane. He could have been with him all along, waiting for the right moment. With clammy hands Carl retrieved his flight bag from the stowaway compartment and glanced at the other passengers. They looked like aliens from another planet—slick, deranged, false, a different species entirely. A young American soldier in tropical civvies and sunshades, a middle-aged pudgy Filipino man, a tense-faced Oriental woman with black hair in a bun: death's impostors, all of them.

In the big warehouselike interior of the Manila airport, guards wore sunglasses and carried guns. The customs officials were rude and snappish. Beyond the counter a mass of people milled around outside, seemingly hundreds or thousands of them. Passing through customs, he saw two doors leading outside—one to the left and one to the right. Not knowing which to take, he angled left.

A short man standing against the wall next to a guard immediately stepped up and took Carl by the arm. "Do you have a hotel reservation?"

Carl's heart lurched. Soldiers were watching. Was it a law that he must have a reservation? Had this been rigged? "No," he said. His muscles tensed to react, but he knew he'd be cut down in any case.

The man pulled a brochure from his pocket and grinned. "Hotel Tropical Paradise. For you I give special deal—twenty-six dollars a night. Okay?"

Carl stared at the man and would have burst out laughing if he had not been so edgy. He felt like a classic hayseed. "How far is it?"

"Close by, very close."

"All right."

The man led him outside into the covered drive where cabs waited and crowds mingled. A car drove up, and the man whisked Carl inside and climbed in after him. There were two men in the front seat, the driver and a young man who looked back and grinned. "Hi. My name is Danny."

Carl tried to smile, but it didn't seem funny anymore. His thoughts clouded with suspicion as the car shot through the crowd and left the airport, entering the swarming streets of Manila. "How far did you say it is?" he asked.

"Oh, very close," Danny said, smiling. "Why you worry so much?"

Carl leaned back and exhaled slowly. He felt at the mercy of these men, of circumstances beyond his control. And he didn't even have a gun.

He became alarmed when they had driven several miles through the crowded streets of Manila with no sign of their destination. Crazily decorated jeepneys roared past with bouncing passengers. Pedestrians crammed the sidewalks, shops, and food stands. Murky liquid stood in the gutters. The hot, oppressive air hung heavily around him. Through the distorted lens of Carl's fatigue, the scene had a nightmarish, otherworldly quality.

He relaxed when the car swung into the secluded drive of a magnificent, sprawling hotel. Carl got out and a well-dressed bellhop fetched his luggage. After paying his escorts, he walked into the palatial lobby and was shown to a room down long corridors with marble checkerboard floors. The room was what a hotel room should be: cool, large, quiet, secluded, with a desk and stationery and a big bed and nice bath. He left his bags there and went back to the lobby.

Raoul, the man who had picked him up at the airport, sat on a sofa by the windows, reading a newspaper. Carl sat beside him and asked about confirming his next-day's flight to Okinawa. Raoul went to the counter and made a quick call. "It's confirmed," he said.

"Thanks." Carl flipped absently through a magazine.

"You want to go somewhere?" Raoul said. "You want a tour of Manila?"

Carl looked up with bleary eyes.

"No," he answered. It would be nice just to lounge around the hotel all day, perhaps even swim.

At that moment four people appeared beside him, a young man and three women, the youngest of whom was strikingly attractive with caramel skin, dark eyes, and long, jet-black hair. The man spoke with Raoul, who turned to Carl and said in a low, gently modulated voice, "Would you like a woman?"

Rather naively perhaps, Carl was startled. He glanced timidly at the three women. The oldest looked at him intensely. The other two looked away.

"No," he said.

"Ah, but you are here for the whole day and night," Raoul said. "Surely you would like a pretty girl?"

Carl felt a hungering loneliness in the pit of his stomach. A dizziness or fatigue or something else overwhelmed him. He closed his eyes and licked his lips. "The young one," he heard himself say.

Raoul spoke rapidly and then everyone vanished

except the girl. Even Raoul left. The girl stood there a moment and then sat down beside Carl, draped one thin leg over the other, crossed her arms in front of her stomach, and looked around the lobby.

"Come on," Carl said, standing.

They went to his room where it was cool and dark. As he bolted the door behind them, he felt a strange trembling in his limbs, a weird element of fear. When he turned back to the room, the girl was sitting on the bed, testing its springiness with her palms. She looked at him with mute, blankly glittering eyes, then kicked off her shoes and lay back.

Carl went into the bathroom and washed his face. Then he phoned room service and ordered two San Miguels, dark. When they came, he poured one for each of them. The girl sipped hers and set it back down on the bedside table.

She could have been sixteen. She could have been twenty. She was thin and dark, and her face had a striking Asian beauty. She wore a short pink dress that buttoned down the front and nylon hose.

He sat for a long time just looking at her. She seemed to feel uncomfortable under his gaze. Finally, when he did nothing, she began to unbutton her dress. He quickly put his hand on hers. "No," he said, shaking his head.

She looked at him questioningly. He watched her, drinking, saying nothing, indicating nothing. She shrugged and stretched out on the bed, waiting.

Carl reached out and touched her brown cheek. She flinched slightly. He wondered what she thought, what she felt. Revulsion? Desire? Greed? Fear? Or nothing at all?

He lay down beside her, stroking her face gently and smoothing her hair. After a long while she sat up and leaned toward him, but he pushed her gently back down, shaking his head. He did not want that. He wanted—warmth? A solace before the storm? He did not know how to name it, but he knew that it was intensely soothing to lie here like this on his side, gently touching the girl, knowing her with just his eyes.

After a while she returned his gaze, and they stared at each other's eyes for a long time. He felt a deep communion with her, but he could not have verbalized what he was thinking. Maybe thinking had nothing to do with it.

After about an hour, he paid her and she left, favoring him with a perplexed smile. He bolted the door behind her and lay down on the bed feeling still lonely but strangely refreshed, like a cactus after a rare rainfall.

● ● ●

In the middle of the night Carl woke in a cold, drenching sweat, his stomach queasy to the point of nausea. He looked around in the darkness, unsure where he was. An evil presence seemed to inhabit the room, but he knew it was from his nightmare. He lay still, reconstructing his life of the past few weeks. New Orleans? Mexico City? Guam? No, Manila, that was it. The thought did not exactly comfort him.

He did not know whether the burning in his bowels was a result of the spicy supper he had eaten or whether it came from plain fear—anxiety, perhaps that was the better word. He leaned over and looked at his watch on the bedside table. Two fifty-five A.M.

The wee hours were the worst. When he woke at such times, he always felt weak, grim, and vulnerable. His life appeared to him in a sickly light, bereft of hope or worth. And now his body clock did not even know whether it was day or night.

He tried to sleep but could not. He turned on the lamp. His experience with the Filipino woman seemed a universe away, a different chapter in his past. He thought of the experience with longing as though she had been a longtime lover instead of a briefly hired companion.

He reached to the table for his butterfly knife, which he kept in his suitcase when in flight. Its presence in his palm gave him comfort. With his thumb he flicked the tang open and casually flipped the knife open and shut, taking it through its revolutions. The action was soothing and unconscious, the click-click a gentle sound. The knife flickered in his hand, gleaming in the lamplight like something living, a pet bird or captive moth.

He froze suddenly, believing he had heard a sound outside his door. Perhaps that was why he had awakened; perhaps his senses had detected something. Chills ran along his body. He lay perfectly still, sweating with fear. He felt like throwing up. Why did he possess no calm? What had happened to his steady-based personality of old, the easy confidence, the strength, the lack of fear, the ability to laugh at danger? He felt like a rabbit paralyzed in headlamps. Maybe it was all the travel. He was an uprooted plant, slowly wilting.

He rose and tiptoed to the door, pressing his ear to it. Nothing. Quickly he unbolted the door and opened it. The corridor was empty, dead. He shut the door and bolted it again.

Sitting on his bed, he practiced the knife routines he had learned so long ago. It was the only tangible remnant of his martial-arts training. He had long since given up the kick-punch routine and concentrated solely on the knife. He was not a fighter or a violent man, but working with the smooth-hinged butterfly gave him a sense of comfort and relieved his stress, channeling it through the fluttering, abstractly fatal movements.

He was not athletic or particularly graceful, and he had never been in a real knife fight, but he could work the butterfly knife like a master—and not just twirl and flip it. Any kid can twirl and flip one with a little practice. A thousand kids stood on street corners flipping their butterfly knives, almost as many as played with nunchakus.

But Carl knew the real moves, the deadly moves, the blocks and strikes and parries and dodges. He had taken that knife training and soared with it, finding the knife a balm to his soul like golf is to others—or crocheting or working crossword puzzles or hunting.

In his idle time he practiced. Sitting in a chair watching television, he played with it. He hated airline flights because he could not keep his knife in his pocket and had to part with it. He knew what hoodlums meant when they described a knife as a mistress. This black-handled, stainless steel darling was his truest lover, gentle as a lamb, swift as a scorpion.

He closed it, set it on the table, and lay back. Wretched, this jet lag. Wretched, everything. He opened a magazine. A brown-skinned woman in a floral sarong with a magnificent scarlet flower tucked behind her ear smiled at him from a full-page ad, holding up a bottle of cologne. He stared at her flat, glossy eyes and felt horribly alone.

CHAPTER 2

● ● ●

A kick sped toward Rick Covey's face at just under the speed of a thirty-eight caliber bullet. Dodging it easily, he stepped in and tagged his opponent with a straight jab to the face. Almost simultaneously his right foot arced up in a sweeping crescent kick and landed across the man's shoulder.

The opponent, grinning at his near demise, stepped back and bowed slightly.

Rick bowed and said, "Next."

Another karate student sprang to his feet, entered the taped-off area, bowed, and began combat with the assistant instructor. Outside the ring, Master Shimabatsu stood with arms crossed, watching impassively.

This student, a powerfully built GI from Kadena Air Base, thought he was tough. He moved in with a flurry of hard front kicks and reverse punches, but Rick parried them with no show of effort and landed a neat hook kick across the back of the man's head. He followed with a light roundhouse kick to the face without ever setting his foot down, then stepped neatly out of the way.

The GI looked like a bull that had just charged through a red cape. He stared at Rick's tall, lightly moving form. Teeth clamped on mouthpiece, gloved hands up, the GI threw a ridgehand. Rick caught it neatly, stepped in, and threw him to the floor. The man landed with a grunt.

The master clapped his hands.

"Line up!" Rick barked.

The twenty or so students lined up, saluted the master and his black belt assistant, and began taking off their belts, making friendly conversation.

Later, in the building's single shower, Rick stood under the cold, hard spray of water that beat against his skin, washing off the sweat. He held his chin up so the water would strike his neck. It always felt good, this cold shower that raised goosebumps on him. He dipped his head under and felt the water stream onto his short, tousled brown hair. Then he cut off the water and stepped out onto the concrete, toweling off. He dressed and, carrying his karate uniform neatly folded, walked out.

The shower was part of a village hotel with small, bare rooms on the top floor of the two-story building, the bottom floor of which served as a dojo or karate training hall. Both the hotel and dojo were owned and run by Master Shimabatsu. Rick was unusual in that he was an American allowed by an Okinawan master to teach karate. In exchange Rick was given room and board and a small wage. He liked it that way. He lived in his Spartan room with a handful of books and magazines, two uniforms, a few changes of clothing, and little else. He shared meals of rice, fish, and vegetables with the master, a taciturn man.

Rick had spent two years as a youth in Okinawa—his father was in the Air Force—acquiring his brown belt at Master Shimabatsu's school. In the States he went on to acquire a second-degree black belt in another style of karate and became an aggressive tournament competitor, winning a number of prestigious titles. But with his wins came disillusionment and the sense that he had lost touch with the true meaning of karate.

Fifteen years after leaving Okinawa, he returned as a tourist and wound up staying to resume his lessons as a brown belt, never telling the master about his stateside honors. He quickly achieved his black belt and was named assistant instructor, a privileged position. As such, Rick ran many of the classes and received private instruction from the master. Classes lasted two hours morning and evening six days a week. In addition, Rick trained with Master Shimabatsu up to three hours every afternoon. Other than that, Rick's time was his own, and he spent it more or less indolently—reading, jogging, swimming in the sea, hiking in the hills, riding his bicycle along mountain roads.

Easygoing, tall, and well-built, Rick was known and respected by both GIs and villagers. Few were the GIs who felt brave enough to want to prove themselves against him. Those who worked themselves up to a challenge, usually abetted by alcohol, found their attack nearly always defused with a word or gesture so gentle it would only have been called karate by the most knowledgeable of martial artists.

The fact was, Rick had not been in an actual fight since he was thirteen, before he had even begun to study karate. But he had fought in innumerable full-contact tournaments, and now he sparred virtually every night in class.

He had the bulky, loose-limbed gait of a big cat, the sort of walk instantly recognizable to men who dabbled in violence, the walk of pure, unsullied, well-founded confidence. But Rick was a friendly fellow who never pressed his advantage unduly, not even against bullish aggressors like the GI he had fought in class. He had defeated countless others like him.

Clean from the shower, he went to his room where a tatami mat lay on the bare floor under a single light bulb. The open window admitted the sounds and smells of the village. He lay on his back and read, turned his light off, and fell into untroubled sleep.

● ● ●

Carrying his beach bag and a cold orange soda, Rick got off the bus, walked across the empty gravel parking area, along the trail that led down the cliff, and out to the white sand beach. No one was in sight—not unusual during the week.

In the warm, salty morning air, Rick finished the drink, set the empty bottle beside his bag, and pulled off his shirt. His deeply tanned arms, chest, and shoulders were massive. The muscles of his stomach formed a hard grid. His constant kicking had developed lean, sinewy legs.

He sat cross-legged on the towel, enjoying the sea breeze and the scenery. The sea looked remarkably blue today in the sunshine. Close to shore its powder-blue and lime-green hues held darker holes of emerald and royal so clear that even from there he could see the forms of sea urchins and coral. Beyond the reef the sea settled into a deep blue.

Rick retrieved his snorkeling gear from the bag. Putting on the flippers, he clomped out into the water, spat in his mask and rinsed it with brine, then blew through the snorkel and glided out into the pleasantly warm water. A short distance from the beach was a hole about seven feet deep, a blue-green bowl surrounded by water two feet deep. He glided over it and hovered, gazing at the spiky sea urchins and small, colorful fish zipping about, looking sideways at their world.

He headed slowly out toward the reef, taking his time to examine the exorbitant world of the inner reef. Fish of every color, including hues that likely never grace the world above, darted about or floated lazily. Sea slugs pretended to be rocks. Coral formed multi-limbed stalagmites like ancient, petrified, skeletal trees in miniature.

Rick stopped abruptly. He saw something. At first he thought it was just a curving line in the sand. Then, he made it out—coming slowly into focus, the body of a sea snake about seven feet long lying in four feet of water. He had never seen one before, but he had heard of them. A person bitten by one could die within seconds. Yet the snakes were said to be utterly passive, could even be handled in relative safety. The occasional human death came when the snakes were caught in fishermen's nets and in panic bit the fishermen.

This one was the color of mottled sand, like the floor it lay on, and its body was as big around as Rick's arm. He could not tell which end was the head and which the tail. The proximity of such a deadly being fascinated him. He became conscious of the sound of his breath in the snorkel tube. A chill ran through him as he tried to comprehend this primitive undersea creature that with a mere movement could end his life. He glided on, slightly shaken.

Farther out he found a crevice perhaps ten feet deep and four feet wide in the shallow sea floor. He liked to follow these ravines, which he saw as arteries leading to a deep, vast heart, channels to the deep where predatory creatures lurked.

Rick, so fearless on land, felt as vulnerable as a husked oyster in the water. Sharks were rarely seen within the reefs, and shark attacks were virtually unheard-of here, but it was not any tangible fear of a specific threat that unsettled him, rather the sense of menace in the sea's unfathomable vastness.

As he followed the ravine out, it deepened and widened, gradually dropping to twenty, thirty, fifty feet—as wide as twenty feet across at the top, where its banks were only about six feet under the surface.

A cold current ran through the chasm, water so clear he could make out every detail of the bottom: strange shells, starfish, and fish bigger than the tiny aquarium-sized ones that puttered about in the shallows, fish as long as his forearm and silvery with stripes like trout, and dense black hulky things that reminded him of groupers.

This ravine cut straight through the reef, an avenue through which big things from the deep sea could travel. He veered away. Ahead, the reef rose in a coral wall to about a foot under the surface. He climbed gingerly onto the sharp coral. It gave him a peculiar sensation to stand up in shallow water half a mile from shore, as though he were walking on water. He warmed himself in the sea breeze, then slipped back down into the ravine. Past the reef it opened out to deep blue. The reef descended like a wall to a depth of perhaps seventy-five feet, where mysterious fish swam. The floor sloped downhill, growing ever deeper as it led unimpeded to the briny deeps.

Rick's many years of karate competition had taught him, with brutal simplicity, to vanquish his fears. One of his trainers, a six-foot-five bruiser who himself was a former full-contact champ, tied Rick to him with a three-foot rope to teach him not to scamper about in the ring. Unable to throw fancy kicks or to slip out of the man's way, Rick had to stand in and punch. He was sorely outclassed, and the bouts became a struggle to master his fear, which mushroomed with each smashing blow. He flinched, ducked, turned, threw his hands up, and finally had to clamp down on his mouthpiece and flail into the heart of the storm. After those sessions his urine was dark with blood.

In college, to test his own endurance, he challenged all black belts in the area to a full-contact sparring marathon wherein he fought each man for three three-minute rounds. The festival of fists and feet lasted seventy-two endless minutes, and Rick won every match.

He learned that survival in the ring, and in life, boiled down to a few basic principles: Don't turn your back, be able to go the distance, train to withstand the hardest blows. And, perhaps most importantly, he learned that even the best of his opponents had just two arms and two legs. Once he mastered this simple arithmetic, his focus shifted, and his entire view of the world changed. It was that realization that propelled him at last into the league of champions.

The sea inspired a different sort of awe in him. It seemed to have no boundaries. He floated a while, enjoying the thrill of being on the brink of the deep sea. Then he turned and, with a sudden flick of his flippers, propelled himself back up the ravine toward the safety of the shore.

CHAPTER 3

● ● ●

Still in a state of shock, Flora opened the door to her house and stared unseeing at the neatly arrayed bamboo furniture. Her four-year-old daughter, Sharon, pushed past her and ran to her room to play. Flora switched on the ceiling fan and sat tentatively in one of the chairs, her black dress stark against the pastel cushion.

The house seemed surreal. Dropping the handkerchief she had been squeezing in both hands, she leaned back with a sigh and closed her eyes. The staccato bark of Sharon's television came to life. Little ones could carry on. The funeral just over, Sharon seemed already to have forgotten the existence of her father. But Flora knew better. At such a young age Sharon's grief would come in spells. Sharon was too young to sustain grief. As for Flora, she was not young enough to elude it.

After her profuse crying, she feared that she looked ugly. Friends would be here soon, and she felt self-conscious. But in fact her eyes had a radiant, rain-washed glitter, dark and gray, and her black dress accentuated the black mane of her hair, contrasting with her pearly skin. Under the cool flow of the ceiling fan she pushed off her shoes and felt the need to weep again. But she had no more tears.

She could only sit there, eyes closed, slouching,

feeling ugly, feeling empty, feeling—what? Nothing. Nothingness. A life to go on with—because, if nothing else, of a little girl.

Flora opened her eyes and stared at the sunny room. Should she take her daughter and move away? It was out of the question for now. Too little money. And yet how could she bear to stay in this house that his presence seemed to inhabit?

The artificial laughter of cartoon characters came from Sharon's TV, the girl laughing along with them. Little Sharon, her rose of Sharon, her darling daughter, her reason for living. Flora wished she could grab her up and hug her and cry, but she did not want to infect her daughter with her own sorrow.

Looking down at the glass-topped coffee table, she stared at the big vase of flowers sent by one of Mac's co-workers. They were wilting already. She needed to add water to the vase to keep them fresh. And when they wilted, what then?

Sharon appeared in the hall doorway. She had her mother's black hair and fair complexion. "Mommy, I'm hungry." Her plaintive little voice reopened the well-springs of Flora's grief. She looked away, putting her hand to her forehead to hide her tears. But Sharon padded across the floor, sat down at her mother's feet, and hugged her legs, rubbing her cheek against the nylon stockings. "It's okay, Mommy."

Flora broke into sobs, and Sharon climbed up and nestled into her mother's lap, comforting her.

● ● ●

Dressed comfortably in jeans and a white cotton blouse, her feet propped on the coffee table, Flora sipped from a cup of hot ginseng tea, her favorite drink, and read the Asian edition of *Time* magazine. With Sharon asleep in her room and Flora's friends all gone, the house was quiet except for the low hum of the ceiling fan. A breeze passing through the screened, louvred windows moved the curtains gently, occasionally bringing her a mild bouquet of Okinawan smells: sea, sewage, motor exhaust, flowers.

Flora reached over and turned on the radio, hoping for some soothing classical music. All she got was harsh Liszt. She changed stations, picked up a manic rock deejay, and turned off the radio with a sigh.

Before her on the coffee table sat a saucer, spoon, and teapot, the green ceramic pot plump and gleaming beside her bare feet. She wiggled her toes with their maroon-painted nails and looked back to the magazine, flipping past world news to the entertainment section: movies, books. If only she could not remember.

A tear slipped down her cheek uninvited. She tried to focus on the magazine. Finally she tossed it onto the table, then leaned over to the small bookcase beside the couch, pulling out her high-school yearbook. She knew she shouldn't do this. It was self-torture. She opened it.

Through her tears she laughed aloud at the sight of the school—mainly Quonset huts—and the grinning principal in a candid shot. An inscription read: "To Flora: Always be the cute, sweet girl that you are today. Carolyn." She tried to remember Carolyn. How many miles had passed under Flora's feet since then, how many seas!

Flora had attended that high school in Okinawa when her father was stationed at Kadena, but after two two-year tours they had gone back to the States. Then she married her high-school sweetheart from Okinawa, Mac Courtier, and returned to the island, where he worked and she taught English to Okinawan students. Irony!

Their son, Harmon, was a senior in high school in the States now, living with Flora's parents. Mac's death had been too sudden for him to come to the funeral. One day fit and healthy, sunbathing on the beach. Next day stone dead. Heatstroke, they said. Harmon was in the middle of finals and could not come, but he would be with Flora during summer break. She understood. He had never been close to his father anyway. They had been more like rivals, surly and uncommunicative.

Flora flipped through the pages, savoring the old pictures, the inscriptions. There was Mac on the football team. He was tough, something of a hood. Hard guy was the parlance back then. She laughed. Mac, hard guy. He had become quite an ordinary person, a man like other men, a good aircraft mechanic, who liked to sprawl in his easy chair after work and watch football games.

Flora pulled a tissue from the box on the coffee table and wiped her face. She drained her teacup and refilled it.

Old Mac, her hero of yore. And she, had she become an ordinary woman? It was possible that in her raven hair there could be found a strand or two of gray, premature, and she wore a few, just a few, more pounds than she should have. But she had never cut her hair short as fashions demanded, having always treasured its long, dark beauty. That and her fair complexion and dark eyes were her prime assets in the realm of physical beauty.

Then there was her buoyant personality. These days she felt about as buoyant as a corpse in the sea. But her inner side manifested itself in the poetry she had written from adolescence on. Flora had notebooks of it—all soft, dreamy, and forlorn. Sometimes an island literary journal published one, and an inspirational magazine in the States had bought some. She wrote about God, lost dreams, departed love, boys marching off to war.

Turning the yearbook pages, she found the picture of Carl, Carl Connolly, her last link to the past. They had been best friends in high school and kept in touch by letters and telephone thereafter. But it had been a while since his last letter. He didn't even know of Mac's death. She needed a friend like him now. She drank her tea, blinking away a fresh batch of tears.

CHAPTER 4

● ● ●

When Carl got off the plane and entered the Naha airport, he did not recognize it. But then, he had not expected to. It had been twenty years since he had been here. This bustling place with lounges and advertisements in no way resembled the forlorn building he had encountered with his parents as a youth.

He hardly cared. He was not here on a trip down memory lane. He passed through customs and walked out front. The parking lot had expanded fantastically. The crowds were unreal. An array of cabs sat out front, painted in the same weird colors as in the old days: purple and yellow, green and orange, blue and pink. He stood there just as he had at Guam, but now there was no savor, just the stunned sense of being adrift in the world.

He approached a cab. "Kadena Circle," he told the Okinawan driver, whose sunglasses reflected the glaring sky.

From there, a commercial and residential area just beyond Kadena Air Base, he would wing it. He had her street number. And if she wasn't here? If she was in the States, on vacation? It had been weeks since they last corresponded. Come to think of it, he owed her a letter. He had not written her since this mess began. He felt disoriented and unbalanced as the cab whisked through the big parking lot, out along the craggy, black-lava coast, and into Naha.

The city at least looked familiar: the same tangle of crowds, signs in Japanese, crazy traffic, curio shops, theaters, strip houses, banks, the works. Naha—the smoggy smell of it, the hot, encroaching feel of it. The driver, true to tradition, drove like a suicidal maniac, honking, veering in and out of traffic, braking suddenly, all with an expression of bored nonchalance.

The cab mounted a freeway that had not existed when Carl was here before, and as they drove north, he caught mere glimpses of areas he had hoped to examine more closely: Machinato, Ojana, Futema, Sukiran, Buckner, Kue, Kadena. In less time than he imagined possible—in the old days fighting traffic on Highway 1 would have taken far longer—he was at Kadena Circle.

The driver looked back, his eyes hidden behind the mirrored lenses. Carl read the address to him. The driver pulled over and shouted to a pedestrian, who leaned into the car and spoke rapidly in Japanese. The driver nodded and drove on, turning onto a side road that led into a residential area.

The road passed between stucco, tile-roofed houses with concrete fences and thick hedges guarding them from view. The cab turned right, down another street, moving slowly as the driver stared out the window at house numbers. He stopped abruptly, backed up, and pulled sharply to the curb, gesturing with his chin at a house on their left. It, like the others, crowded behind a low wall and dense flame-leaf bushes.

"Wait here," Carl said, getting out. He checked the number from his address book, then walked up the steps that led into the yard, went to the front door and, with a palpitating heart, knocked.

The door opened and Flora peeked out sleepily, as though just wakened from a nap. "Carl?" She frowned, stepping out. "Carl?" Drowsiness vanished from her face.

Carl just stood there, his face consumed by a wide grin.

"But what—?" Her confusion displaced by a welcoming smile, she hugged him.

"Wait," he said after a few moments. "I've got to pay the cab."

He paid the driver and fetched his luggage. Flora led him into the house. The living room showed a breezy comfort—bamboo furniture, house plants, open windows, a ceiling fan. Wrinkled sofa cushions indicated where she had been napping. This was the home she had described so many times in her letters.

"You knew, then," she said, hugging him again as he set down his bags.

"Knew what?"

"About Mac." She stared at him. "About Mac dying."

"What? No, I didn't know."

She eyed him doubtfully, as though he were making a poor joke. "You had to know, Carl."

"No, really."

"Then why are you here? I mean . . ." She released her hold. "I called your office, but they said you were gone indefinitely."

"What happened?"

"Heatstroke, they said. Last Sunday." She began to cry and he pulled her to him. "But you knew," she said. "Some part of you knew. Things happen that we don't know anything about, Carl."

His eyes followed her as she walked to the coffee table for a tissue. She was still in good shape after all these years, still attractive. He was glad to see that. He wondered how well-preserved he looked. He felt frazzled, dirty, and tired.

She sat on the sofa, trying to steady her erratic breathing, and he sat in a chair.

"Sit beside me," she said. He did, and she took his hand.

"Tell me about Mac," he said.

She sighed. "We spent Saturday afternoon at the beach. Sunday he was late getting up. See, usually I get up and get my bath and when I get out he's already up eating breakfast with Sharon. Well, when I got out of the tub he still wasn't up." Her voice rose as she struggled not to cry again. "When I went in to see about him, he was dead."

"Oh, Flora."

"I screamed. He was cold, Carl. I don't know how long he had been dead."

"So it was heatstroke from the sun?"

"I guess. That's what the doctors said." She blew her nose. "Can we talk about this later? I'm sorry."

"Sure. I'm sorry." He looked around. "Where's Sharon?"

"Preschool. She gets home at three." She leaned her head on his shoulder. "Thank you for coming, Carl. I don't know what to do."

"It's all right now." He lightly stroked her hair with his free hand. "Your hair is still gorgeous."

She laughed. "I've got some gray. I counted three hairs. Can you believe it?"

"I've got more than that in my beard. I tried growing a beard, and it was salt and pepper."

"Really?" She stared at his face, put her hand out, and stroked his cheek. "I bet it looks good." She paused. "Oh, Carl," she said with sudden realization, "what's the matter? Why are you here?"

He wondered whether he should tell her. But what other plausible reason could he invent for his unexpected visit? He sighed with fatigue. "I was told to leave."

"Not fired?"

He shook his head. "I put too much heat on the

wrong guy in a story I did. I was told I'd better leave town."

"But you've been told that before, haven't you?"

"This time it was from somebody who wouldn't say it if it weren't true. They've got a contract out on me, Flora. And they're the kind of people who don't mind traveling to settle their debts."

"You think they followed you here?"

"We left them a trail a bloodhound couldn't follow. My editor arranged it. I've got tickets zigzagging from New Orleans to here and on to Singapore, Jakarta, all kinds of places. Right now I'm en route to some other country. Let them spend their fortune in airline tickets."

He didn't mention the mix-up in Guam. It had to have been an accidental snafu. No way could someone have tampered with international ticketing or influenced his travel agent, with whom he had dealt for years. Instead, it seemed to him as though the world at large was conspiring with his enemies, throwing obstacles in his path to confuse him while they moved in.

"Oh, Carl, are you sure you're not in danger? Seriously?"

"Seriously. My itinerary was carefully arranged and kept in complete secrecy."

"Who's paying for all your tickets?"

"The newspaper. They gave me an extended leave of absence."

"Oh, Carl, this sounds terrible, terrible."

"Now I didn't want to get you upset. There is absolutely no danger, not a hint of it. Hear me? This is a free vacation as far as I'm concerned. I always wanted to come see you here. This was a perfect time to do it."

She relaxed slightly. "Are you sure?"

He smiled reassuringly. "Of course. It's perfect. I've come when you needed me, and you're here when I need you."

"As always."

"As always. I'll get a hotel room, and—"

"No! You'll stay here, of course. There's room."

"No, really."

"Really!"

"What about your neighbors?"

"Neighbors?" She frowned, then laughed. "Oh, silly! I'll just say you're my brother if anyone asks, but they won't. And besides, that's nearly the truth, isn't it?"

"Yes." He squeezed her hand.

She leaned her head against his shoulder. "Carl, I'm so glad you've come. I didn't know what I was going to do. I thought I'd die. And I have to keep up a strong front for Sharon. Harmon won't be here till this summer. I don't know what to do, go back, or—"

"Just don't worry about it for a while, okay? You need some time to recover. You don't need to be making any decisions now. We'll just have a vacation, all right?"

"But there are so many decisions. You don't know."

"I don't care. You've got to rest. Let's put a moratorium on anything except the essentials for the next few days."

"I've canceled my classes all next week. After that I've either got to go back or quit."

"All right. We'll worry about that then."

"I'm so glad you're here. You can't imagine."

Carl leaned his head back against the sofa. Always the unexpected. Mac's death had unbalanced him anew. Okinawa and Flora rekindled memories of his youth, memories of times so young and sweet and full of woe.

CHAPTER 5

● ● ●

Memories. On a Friday afternoon when he was thirteen, Carl Connolly was spared an innocuous adolescence when his mother summoned him downstairs. He was in his room. Who could remember what he had been doing? Talking on the phone? Staring out the window? Looking at his posters of Clint Eastwood, Marlon Brando, and Steve McQueen?

He came downstairs and entered his grandmother's room. Grandma was sitting on the edge of the bed with a stunned expression on her normally placid face. Mother, however, looked pale and wasted, her face puffy from crying. She was folding her clothes. Grandma left the room and closed the door.

"Carl, your dad and I are separating," Mother told him tersely.

He stared at her, not really comprehending. "Why?"

She didn't look at him. "We're having problems communicating."

In inverse reaction to the turmoil that obviously raged within his mother, Carl felt suddenly quite calm and mature. He sat on the edge of the bed and crossed one leg over the other. "Well," he said in the manner of a counselor, "maybe it's for the best."

His mother leaned over and hugged him, crying

silently. She told him she would always love him and promised she would not be separated from him for long. Carl smiled paternally as he patted her back.

It took a while to hit. Perhaps that is the way it will be when the end of the world comes, he reflected much later. We will stare uncomprehending at a sky that begins to fracture, revealing behind it something we could never have imagined.

Carl cried constantly for the next two days. Then it was Sunday night and time for church—he had been permitted to skip the morning services—and he could not very well cry in church. So his mother, a nurse, gave him a Valium, and off they went: Dad, grim and tense; Grandma, silent and baffled; Mother, her face drawn; and Carl, trying not to cry as he stared out the car window at the skoshi cabs that whisked by. A steady drizzle blurred his view.

At the church in Ojana he sat with Flora and her boyfriend, Thomas. Rather than the continued hysteria he had expected, he began to feel nonchalant. His tight muscles began to relax. As the preacher spoke from the podium, Carl felt himself almost laugh inside. So his parents were splitting up, so what? Big deal. For the first time since the initial blow, he felt a sense of detachment.

Flora, to whom he had described the calamity already on the phone, was extremely attentive to him. Showing surprise at the calm he began to exude, she held his hand in a sisterly show of support. Thomas shouldn't mind. Carl and Flora were best friends, not sweethearts.

But after a while Carl released her hand. He didn't need mothering. The impenetrable aura of the faces on his bedroom wall—cowboy Clint, biker Marlon, POW McQueen—suffused him. He understood now what it was like to be tough and uncaring inside. The depth of his previous grief amused him.

By the end of church service the Valium had taken

full effect. Carl no longer felt concerned that tomorrow his mother would go to the Naha airport and depart for the States, leaving him here for the next year or so with Dad and Grandma.

All that weekend Carl had thought nostalgically of his now-gone happy childhood. He remembered their cozy home in the States and the way the family watched "Bonanza" in the den Sunday nights after church. That was a good time, an innocent time, a paradise lost. Now he did not know what to do. He was adrift in a lawless cosmos.

But Sunday night, buffered by Valium, he dismissed such thoughts as sentimental claptrap and readjusted his outlook. Come Monday morning, when he went to school, he would be a different person, no longer the vacuous child. Now he could truly say that he had suffered.

Like Clint Eastwood's mysterious cowboy, he had a secret tragedy to conceal behind an impassive demeanor. Emotions no longer meant anything to him. He would squint and care for nothing and be unmoved. His eyes would reflect, to the perceptive observer, the depths of suffering he had known.

But by Monday the Valium had worn off. All crumpled and weepy inside, he stood waiting for the bus with neighborhood kids, trembling lest he break down and cry in public.

● ● ●

Carl could not put his finger on the moment when he and Flora had become friends. Perhaps it had been during the school play. He played the villain, a role he relished. She took care of the props. The cast practiced after school, then waited for rides home.

One foggy evening when it was nearly dark, a few of them stood outside under a streetlamp, waiting for their parents. Carl and Flora, casual friends, began to talk. At first it was just chat, but they quickly warmed to each other, perceiving one another's sensitivity and capacity for suffering. Since they had no romantic designs on each other, they did not feel inhibited as they otherwise might have. Carl was developing a crush on Rosette, one of the actresses, though he had not revealed it to anyone yet, least of all Rosette. And Flora was involved with Thomas.

Carl would always remember that scene under the streetlamp. They stood away from the others, and the misty light made Flora's long, blue-black hair unusually lustrous, contrasting with her pale complexion and dark eyes.

After that they began to exchange notes and phone calls, and somehow, sometime, they began to use the word *love*. They both knew what they meant, so it was a safe love and could be verbalized often. They closed their notes with "I love you" and said it on the phone as the standard ending to their conversations. They found deep pleasure in using those words.

To talk on the phone late at night they developed a special timing. She agreed to call him at ten-thirty on the dot. Lying in his dark room, he put his phone in bed with him, carefully watching the luminous clock, his hand resting lightly on the phone. At ten-thirty, at the first hint of a ring, he picked up the receiver. No one else heard it ring.

CHAPTER 6

● ● ●

Sharon looked at her mother, then at Carl. "Uncle Carl," she said, "will you say grace?"

He smiled rather grimly. They bowed heads and he mumbled a prayer. Then Flora reached for the big platter of chicken and handed it to him while Sharon grabbed for the rolls.

"She looks so much like you," Carl told Flora. He smiled down at the dark-haired girl. "You're such a pretty girl, Sharon."

"Say thank you," her mother coached.

"Thank you." Sharon smeared butter on the hot roll.

"Did you see Sharon's drawing? The one she did at preschool today? The teacher said it showed a lot of talent. Sharon got an A."

"An A? That's great."

Carl sipped his iced tea and relaxed in the bright, homey dinette where they were eating. Fine Noritake china graced a clean, white linen tablecloth. They ate baked chicken with almonds and rice and green peas and a casserole with green beans and water chestnuts.

After supper Sharon lay on the living room floor and colored in a coloring book while Carl sat in a chair and Flora on the sofa, both drinking ginseng tea. The radio played classical music softly.

Carl stared into space. "Okinawa seems so different," he said.

"Have you been around? To Kadena? To Kue?"

"I haven't been anywhere. I came straight from the airport here."

"I'll bet a lot has changed. Like the freeway. That would be new."

"I couldn't believe it."

"Oh, there were so many changes after Japan took over. So many more people now, more congestion, more traffic. But a lot of it's still the same, still Okinawa."

"Okinawa," he mused. He slipped off his shoes and, like Flora, propped his feet on the coffee table. "Do you still play the guitar?"

With a smile she got up, walked down the hall, opened a closet, and returned with a wide-necked guitar with nylon strings. Turning off the radio, she sat down, tucked a foot under her leg, and strummed a G chord. Her long fingernails made the chording awkward, but that was nothing new.

"Do you remember this?" she asked. Clearing her throat, she sang, "Tears cried in vain, what could be sadder?" Her soft, lilting voice was not that of a singer but still pretty. "Blind of the tears, what could be madder?"

Yes, he remembered. It was a song she had written long ago, one of his favorites. The tune was simple, the words dreamy and romantic. Her poems had always seemed a bit sentimental to him, even the ones she wrote for him. If he cared for poetry at all it was for the crisp, unsentimental types like the poems of Ted Hughes and Robert Penn Warren.

He had written a few poems back then, and she put one or two to music. His poems had been more symbolic, heavily influenced by Bob Dylan. The images were cryptic and bizarre, but the tone—intense loneliness—rang out clearly.

"That's beautiful," he said when she finished. Entranced by the music, the hot tea, the company, he suspected he would sleep deeply and long tonight. "Do you remember 'Outside the Law'?"

She smiled and fetched a notebook from the closet. "I've saved them all, you know," she said. "All our poems and notes." She leafed through it and took out a page.

"May I see that?"

Handing him the notebook, Flora began strumming a fast-paced song in E. "Outside the Law" was a poem he had written at age fourteen, and she had put it to music. Almost intuitively she had picked the fast pace and harsh tone the words required. Browsing through the notebook, he listened as she sang:

> "A *fence of toys towers skyward;*
> *There is a costume-jewelry store*
> *To keep the people deeply occupied,*
> *To keep them away from the door.*"

Carl reddened at the childish clumsiness of his lyrics. Flora went on:

> "*Now the hunter has been outlawed,*
> *In desolation he must remain.*
> *Lonely hours he spends in the forest,*
> *Wondering whether he is insane.*
>
> "*Sequined serpents serve as tempters,*
> *He can hear their lusty call,*
> *But now he knows it's much too late*
> *When he's living outside the law.*"

Sharon's voice interrupted. "Mommy, I'm out of purple," she said.

"Hush, Mommy's singing," Flora said, still strumming.

Carl leaned back and closed his eyes, remembering the poem and the feelings that had engendered it, remembering the Flora of old taking it and fashioning the music for it and then, as a surprise, playing it for him.

As she sang, he drifted off into memories. He pictured the basement room of her house where they often went to talk and listen to records. He saw Flora, wearing black slacks and a white satin blouse, so perfect with her own coal-and-snow colors. They chatted in the cozy lamplight, and then she played the guitar and sang.

After Flora ended the song, the room was quiet except for the hum of the ceiling fan. Carl dared not open his eyes lest he be confronted by the present. He became acutely conscious of the sound of Sharon's crayon scraping the paper. When he opened his eyes, they were so wet he could not focus. He felt he must either laugh or cry. He shook his head and laughed, trying to dispel the lack of control that threatened him. "Great," he managed in a shaky voice.

Flora smiled demurely and looked down at the guitar, plucking its strings at random. "I thought you were brilliant," she murmured. "I still do."

He laughed again. "That poem's so clumsy, and it's pure Dylan." He paused. "But I tell you, Flora, if I were to write it again today, I don't think I could put it any plainer."

"That's what I mean."

"Mommy, I'm out of purple," Sharon said again, a hint of resentment in her voice.

Flora put the guitar aside and sat on the floor beside her daughter. "What needs to be purple?" she asked. "We'll see what we can do with what we've got."

CHAPTER 7

● ● ●

"The double-arm trap." Master Shimabatsu nodded to Rick, who stepped back with a downward block and shouted. The master shouted in response, and Rick stepped forward with a punch.

With the speed and tenacity of a praying mantis, Shimabatsu trapped Rick's punching arm between his own forearms. He froze the movement so Rick could observe it. Then, with an alarming rush of power, he stepped backward and swept Rick in a circle to the floor. Rick landed hard, not expecting the throw, but rolled with it and took the impact on his open palm. He stood up, straightened his uniform, and nodded.

"Again," said the master.

This time there was no hesitation. Shimabatsu trapped his arm and threw him. Prepared, Rick rolled deftly and returned quickly to his feet.

Now it was Rick's turn. The master punched. Rick, frowning, stepped aside and seized the arm between his forearms. He stepped back to throw him, but the master stood immobile, his expression blank. Rick adjusted his grip to apply pressure just below the elbow, and suddenly the master's stance yielded. Despite his age, the master fell with such agility that he scarcely seemed to touch the floor, rolling instantly to his feet.

After several tries, Rick began to get the hang of it. It was a matter of leverage and positioning. Depending on the amount of pressure applied, the opponent could be merely thrown, or his arm could be snapped in two at the elbow.

"All right," said Shimabatsu. "Enough practice now. Supper soon."

They bowed to one another, and Rick hurried upstairs to change. Later he joined the master in a small room adjoining the kitchen where they sat on mats at a low table and ate fish, rice, and vegetables with chopsticks and sipped from cups of hot green tea.

After supper Rick went for a stroll. He liked to walk around the village of Jagaru before the evening class began. It was the cool of the day, though still humid. The houses, gardens, and gravel road took on rich hues in the deep shade. A water buffalo stood in a field, tethered to a tree. Rick smelled the smoke of cooking from the houses and the remaining odor of the "honey cart" that had come that day, selling human sewage for fertilizer. Appalling to him so many years before, now the smell registered as neither good nor bad, merely a smell.

He turned onto a small path that led uphill through the woods and out into a patch of deep grass, brilliant in the late sunlight. The trail rose steeply to the crest of a hill. From the top he commanded a view of the sea to the west. Below him the trees hid the village except for an occasional rooftop, but beyond them he saw the rim of the sea and the mute statement of the sunset. Rick sat cross-legged on a stone and soaked in the warm beauty of the sinking sun.

From a house below he heard the plink of a koto. The sound of that instrument was rare in villages nowadays. It was more common to hear a radio spouting irreverent modern music. The soothing, traditional music recalled to his mind images he had once held of the mystery of the Orient. Even the sounds of traffic hushed as if all the hustle and bustle of the modern age had paused to hear the single lonely koto.

Rick imagined its player, some gentle-faced, kimono-clad Okinawan woman kneeling on the floor of her house, stroking the catgut strings with long, delicate fingers spiked with plectrums. The twangings were spare, bereft of the fullness found in so much of the world's music. The koto played a music of understatement; it did not gush like flamboyant waterfalls and ostentatious vegetation; rather, it seemed lean and uncluttered like rock or bone.

The minor-keyed song was unforgiving and full of woe. It told the story behind the form, the violence that underlies the practiced punch, the ages of life and death that had existed in these island hills.

Rick felt a wave of sadness come over him, haunted by all the years of his life that were gone. What had he done with them? What was he doing with them? Was he pouring them out like water? A karate bum, living a simple, Spartan life in a remote village.

At first he had idealized his lifestyle, comparing himself to the old Shaolin monks of China, but now he just existed. If he grappled with anything in life it was with the severe demands of karate technique—that and nothing else. To learn and master the double-arm trap and then to go on and learn another and another technique, ever returning to the basics. Another kata, another weapon. It was a life as empty as an unused pot. The artistry was something to admire, perhaps, but the vessel served no purpose. It merely sat there, deaf to the lively voices surrounding it.

He realized the sun had set, its grandiose display fading. The sea lay like a strip of iron under the luminous sky. The trees stood black in the dusk. The music stopped. He heard the swish of traffic far away on the highway and voices down in the village like tinkling chimes.

A young Okinawan couple strolled out of the grove below him. This hill was a popular overlook for locals. Rick stood politely to defer to them. They smiled and bowed. He returned the gesture and headed down the hill. At the edge of the woods he turned and looked back. The couple sat side by side on the stone where he had been, oblivious to the beauties of the dusk. Their heads leaned toward one another, and the girl smiled broadly as the young man told her secret and wonderful things.

CHAPTER 8

• • •

"Recognize that house?"

Carl looked at the two-story house built against the hill. Ivy crawled along the brick. "Yeah," he said. It was Flora's old house. They were parked at the curb, motor idling, lost in reverie. Flora gently put the car in gear and they cruised on, down to Kue.

At the sight of the hospital there, Carl's insides lurched with nostalgia. "Well, the hospital could not contain the pain," he remembered having written, "and the PX could not support the joy."

The hospital lawn stretched to their left as she drove. "Of all the cigars bought, and the prescriptions picked up, I had thought there might have been something of worth," the poem had continued. The silent words dripped in the cave of his mind. "Oh, remember the chapel organ and the theater and the water tank where timelessness appeared."

Flora had put those words of his to a melancholy tune, slow and bluesy but with a dispassionate rather than sentimental touch.

She headed the car into the residential area.

Carl could not believe what he was seeing: the same street, the same duplexes and quadruplexes that had been here when he was a youth. A curious, hallucinatory feeling swept through him.

"That's where Patti Day lived," he said. "My first girlfriend here." He remembered brown-haired, tanned Patti, all of twelve years old, in cutoff jeans, sitting on a wall tapping the soles of her bare feet against the brick. He had sat beside her wearing mirror sunglasses, quite the young antihero. "Back there was where Rick lived." Carl pointed.

"Who was he?"

"You didn't know Rick? Sure you did. He was my best friend. I guess that was before you and I hung out together. We played basketball over behind the barracks." He chuckled fondly. "I haven't seen him since I left."

He remembered walking to the PX with Rick, crossing the wide hospital lawn, jumping the benjo ditches filled with sewage, going into the little store where a cold-eyed Okinawan woman presided behind the counter.

The houses passed by slowly. He was lost, utterly lost in time like an asteroid drifting through the cosmos, visiting and revisiting ancient vacuums.

Carl sat forward and pointed. "Look, that's where Brenda lived. I had a crush on her but never had the guts to tell her. Five months later somebody told me she had had a crush on me. We both liked each other, but neither of us knew. When I found out, I asked her for a date, but she didn't have a crush on me anymore."

"When was all this?"

"Before I met you," Carl assured her. "The year before."

"Did she go out with you?"

"Yeah. We went to a movie. Thirty-five cents, it cost." He laughed. "They used to not let me in because my hair was too long. Almost touched my collar, radical for those days. So I'd wet it down to make it look short."

She laughed. "I know. They wouldn't let me in one

time because my dress was too short. It made me so mad."

"All the girls wore short dresses back then, didn't they?"

Flora nodded absently. "I can't believe our parents let us dress like that."

"The fad, I guess." Carl looked off to the right. "That's where Shelley lived."

"I remember her."

"Another fiasco—one of many."

"Poor Carl." They both laughed. As they reached the end of the curving road, Flora stopped to turn around.

"On the other side of that fence over there is Jagaru," Carl said. "That's where I took karate."

"I didn't know you took karate."

"I took about three classes and quit. Rick and I took it together, but he stuck with it. I took it again later when I got back to the States."

"So you're a karate expert, huh?"

"No, I quit there, too. Let's go by Jagaru later, okay? I'd at least like to drive by the dojo."

They headed back up the street. When they got to his cove, she turned down it slowly. Up ahead he saw the quadruplex where he had lived. He almost expected to see the old Datsun Bluebird sitting in their parking spot.

"That's where Vicki lived." He motioned to the residence two doors down from his. "She and I went steady right after I got here. She was two years older than I."

"Such a ladies' man," she teased.

She stopped, and he stared at the building, at the door beside which his father's nameplate had hung. A thousand memories besieged him, clamoring for his attention all at once: sitting on the roof with Rick, necking with Vicki in the utility room, playing football on the open lawn beside the buildings, sitting around the swing set with neighborhood boys and girls, shooting baskets with Rick on the court behind the GI barracks.

"I wish we could go inside," he said.

"We could knock and ask."

"No." They sat in silence, the motor off. A group of tots played on the sidewalk. The realization that life still went on here, that children still grew up in this neighborhood just as he had grown up, gave him a feeling of personal worthlessness, that all the experiences that were so precious to him were like grains of sand on the beach. A sense of loss overwhelmed him.

"I remember when I first came back here," said Flora. "I felt the same as you do—all the nostalgia, all the memories. But then I got used to everything again, and now it's just like home. I guess if I ever go back to the States, I'll get nostalgic again."

Carl broke into a short, rueful laugh. "Well, let's go before we see a ghost."

She smiled sadly. "There aren't any ghosts." She started the engine.

When they reached Jagaru, Carl leaned forward suddenly. "That's it. That's the dojo," he said, and she stopped the car in front of a nondescript, gray, two-story building. "I wonder if anybody's in there."

"Well, why don't you go look?"

He thought a minute. "All right. Want to come?"

She shook her head. "I'll wait here."

He got out, crossed the road, and stepped into the cool, dark room, bowing automatically. Two men were working out. They turned and looked. One was Oriental, no doubt the master—not that Carl would recognize him. The other was a tall, tanned, muscular American with curly brown hair.

The American took a step toward him. "Can I help you?" His voice had a slightly overbearing edge as though he did not care to be bothered just now.

"No, I was just looking."

The man seemed to await further explanation.

"I used to take karate here a long time ago," Carl said, feeling uncomfortable. "Not for long, though."

"Well, you're welcome to look around. Class starts at seven if you're interested."

Carl bowed slightly but did not notice whether the man bowed back. The master had barely spared him a glance. Immediately the two men resumed their practice.

Carl looked around at the bare wooden floor, the single full-length mirror, the black-and-white photos on the wall. He remembered himself and Rick showing up for their first lesson, both cocky youngsters dressed in stiff, new, cotton uniforms with white beginner's belts. The room had smelled—as it did now—of tension and sweat.

Distracted by his thoughts of karate glory, he had not noticed many details at the time. He knew, vaguely, that the dojo was run by a stern Okinawan man. Sometimes high-ranking students, including American servicemen, ran the class.

Carl had not even been good at the basic stretching exercises. During one exercise a violent cramp had seized his calf, and he stopped to massage it. The American instructor stared at him fiercely and demanded to know why he had quit. Mortified, Carl tried to explain. But the instructor didn't seem impressed.

Carl had had little concept of what karate was all about. The only thing he knew for sure was that there was a devastating technique called the chop, the karate chop. He knew it was devastating because he had seen it on TV. On spy shows like "The Man from U.N.C.L.E." he saw the hero chop the bad guy on the neck so that the bad guy fell down unconscious. To Carl that was karate.

Essentially, then, he had taken up karate to learn that chop so that the next time a bully menaced him, Carl could whack him on the neck. The bully would then fall down, and Carl would become a rugged hero, feared by boys and admired by girls. During the class's free period, he stood in front of the mirror throwing chop after chop at his own image. His interest didn't last, however, and after a few lessons he quit. Rick remained an enthusiastic student.

Years later Carl had enrolled at a dojo in the States. He studied there for a year and made friends with a higher-belt student whose specialty was the butterfly knife. That student introduced Carl to the weapon, which quickly displaced Carl's rudimentary interest in karate.

He quit the school but practiced knife work with the student, purchasing books and charts on it. He was even able to acquire a copy of an unpublished paper diagraming a kata involving the butterfly knife, a paper to which only black belts were supposed to have access. From that his comprehension of the weapon had grown exponentially.

He glanced at the short Okinawan master. Of course he would not remember Carl. Carl felt rather foolish for coming here. He turned to go, remembered to bow—though the two men ignored him—and went out.

"See anything interesting?" Flora asked.

"No." He got in. "I barely remembered it. Let's go up this way. It's a pretty drive."

"I never go up these back roads anymore," Flora lamented as they drove the narrow, winding road into the hills. "You know, it's funny, but it's been ages since I've just been riding. Mac and I never went anywhere. Seems like the only places I go are to work and shopping. And church, of course."

"I can't remember where this comes out, but I guess we'll find out."

"Good. I feel like getting lost."

CHAPTER 9

● ● ●

Carl sat up in the middle of the night, suddenly wide awake. Something in his mind was coming into focus, something unreal, suspended in the realm between past and present. Rick Covey. His face loomed in Carl's mind—the tousle-haired kid he had known—but his face was different, older. It had a strong, aquiline appearance. Carl visualized him so clearly. Yes, yes!

Carl sprang out of bed. What time was it? Two-thirty. Charged with excitement, he dressed, went from the guest bedroom into the kitchen, and poured himself some water. Then he sat on the living room sofa and switched on a lamp. It cast a pleasant glow in the still house.

Rick Covey. He no longer felt certain. When he had awakened, it was as though his brain had kicked out an answer to an unasked question. Some part of his mind, having deliberated in secret, had told him that the American man in the karate dojo was Rick. He was certain of it.

But now, awake and more rational, he was skeptical. Carl had lost all contact with Rick after leaving Okinawa. The chances of that man being Rick were infinitesimal. It was a trick of the memory, a distortion caused by half-remembered circumstances.

He heard a sound in the house, and for one electric, instinctual moment he reached for the butterfly knife in his pocket. Then he realized the sound was Flora stirring in her room. In a few moments she padded out, sleepy-eyed, wrapped in a floor-length Oriental robe, her hair rumpled. She squinted in the light. "Couldn't sleep, huh?" she said.

"I just woke up."

She sat in a chair. "I have trouble sleeping, too." She stared glumly at the portrait of her son hanging on the wall. Dressed in a suit and with tight curly hair, Harmon grinned out from a photographer's backdrop of blue velvet. "What woke you? Jet lag?"

"I was just thinking. I had an idea. I can't decide if it's crazy or not."

"Well, tell me what it is."

He leaned forward. "In that dojo today there was a guy—well, he looked an awful lot like my old friend Rick Covey. You know, the one I told you about. We took karate there together for a while. But I don't see how it could be him. I don't think it's possible."

"Why not?"

"It just seems so unlikely."

"It probably seems unlikely for me to be living here, too, but here I am."

"That's true."

"Want something to drink? Fruit punch?"

"No thanks."

Flora went into the kitchen, and the pale glow of the refrigerator light suffused the darkness of the kitchen doorway. It slid away and she appeared with a glass of red liquid, like the colored sugar-water in a humming-bird feeder. "Well, why don't you go back there and ask him?" she said, leaning against the doorjamb.

"Ask him if he's Rick Covey?"

"Yes."

"What if he's not?"

"Then he beats you up, and I come visit you in the hospital."

He laughed. "I just can't decide. Something tells me it was him, but really I don't see how it can be."

"And that's what woke you at two in the morning."

"Sorry if I disturbed you out here."

"Oh, I was awake already."

"I might go back there in the next few days."

"Don't be silly. Go tomorrow. I'll take you, or you can take the car and go by yourself."

He thought it over. The belief that it might really be Rick rekindled his excitement. "All right. I will."

"Good. Now I think I'm going back to bed. I need some rest even if I don't get to sleep."

"Just relax and don't worry about anything."

She laughed at his parental tone and took the glass back into the kitchen. "Good night," she said, heading back to her room. "Don't stay up all night thinking about it or you'll be tired tomorrow."

"All right."

She returned to her room, and he heard the creak of her bed, the sound of shifting covers.

Another nagging thought sprouted the seeds of wakefulness: that thrill of fear at the noise he heard when Flora got up. Did he still fear a hit? Could his trail possibly have been followed? The shadows in the room looked unfriendly. The balmy island night seemed anything but peaceful.

But he thought of Rick and shook his fear off. Maybe the instructor would be Rick. Maybe, maybe not. He switched the lamp off and went back to the guest room.

● ● ●

Threats don't necessarily mean anything. Carl learned that in the journalism business. A staff writer for a New Orleans newspaper, he had confronted angry politicians and covered stories in rough parts of town. He used to worry about it. He'd had night calls, been threatened with lawsuits—even violence. But one night he had the inspiring realization that unless his enemies were actually coming to kill him, he need not worry. And if they were coming to kill him, he could deal with that, too.

Naturally hardened to the occasional adversity he encountered in his routine duties, he knew how to be tough when he needed to, and he knew how to turn on a warm, inviting persona to lure stories from the recalcitrant. Tricks of the trade. He'd come to regard the usual tough guy with detachment, even contempt.

Then he hit a trail involving investigation of the drug underworld. This crowd did not consist of the usual big-talking politicians or bureaucratic bluffers. These fellows, he was told, played hardball.

At first, things had gone smoothly. He came on soft and friendly, and people talked. He amassed information, which made for good investigative news reporting.

Weeding through the usual quota of nonsense, he began to discern an intriguing trend: a number of the suspects had business connections with an import-export merchant in a seedy business district. This merchant's son was a minor city official. The evidence began to mount. Unable to contact the official, Carl called the old man.

The call set off a conflagration involving the editors and attorneys of the newspaper. At first the man threatened lawsuits. But Carl could substantiate all his allegations, and his editors were hard-nosed and prepared to print.

The merchant, to everyone's surprise, dropped out of sight. Word was, he had left the country after putting a contract out on Carl.

The reporter who had once sneered at the thought of being threatened now seriously began to wonder if and when he would be killed. He brought the matter to his editors, who acted with startling alacrity. Carl was frankly surprised at their eagerness to protect him. Similar situations had come up before, albeit rarely, he learned.

Only two or three editors were involved with the details of the plan. In less than a week Carl had packed his bags and gone on an extended, round-the-world journey.

Carl took pleasure in imagining some meathead hit man struggling past customs officials in every flyblown country in Southeast Asia looking for a target that wasn't there. But he didn't bet the rent on his immunity. There was always the chance that his stalker could wise up and backtrack, or that he had been on to him all along and was taking his time to do a special job. Still, it was a big world in which to find one small reporter.

So while he did not give much conscious thought to the situation, a part of him was still on hold, on alert, reacting like a sleeping cat to the sound of a heavy footstep.

● ● ●

Thoughts of violence triggered violent memories, like the night-time class party at an officers' club he and Rick had attended.

After supper, they had gone for a walk. They rounded the corner of the building to the big parking lot where street lamps glowed with a sickly aura. They stopped suddenly. A cluster of school toughs leaned against a wall, smoking cigarettes. Carl wished they could turn back, but it would be obvious they were afraid. Besides, Rick seemed unaware of the danger they were approaching.

One of the toughs stepped out, a cigarette in his mouth. "Well, well," he said. "Look who's here, an egghead and a dork."

Rick looked up with a flash of anger, suddenly aware of the hoods. Carl's stomach fluttered; he knew this guy practiced karate. Carl and Rick had not yet taken up the art.

Anger flashed in Rick's eyes. "What'd you say?" he challenged.

"I said dork," the guy repeated. He stepped forward and threw a kick at Rick's groin. Carl watched the motion in disbelief. It seemed so slow, yet unstoppable. The toe of the boy's shoe caught Rick hard in the abdomen.

Rick grunted with the impact and, fierce as a bull, sprang forward and began punching his assailant in the face. The tough, all his karate training deserting him suddenly, put his hands up blindly to ward off the blows. Rick got in some good licks. The other boys stood back and a few girls crowded around. Rick pushed his opponent against the wall and continued to pummel his head and body.

"All right, all right." The hood surrendered, bent over, his arms shielding his face.

At last Rick quit and stepped back.

Like an audience waiting for the curtains to open, everyone stared at the tough. As he lowered his arms, a collective gasp responded to the trail of blood under his nose and the raised welt over one eye. He spat a mixture of saliva and blood onto the pavement and coughed with a sobbing sound. "All right," he hacked.

"Just watch who you call a dork," Rick warned.

The boy did not look at him and did not straighten up. His friends seemed awed that their karate hero had been thrashed by Rick, whose only tools had been fists and blind rage. The seemingly magic power of a karate kick had been rendered ineffective by pure anger—not to mention bad aim on the kicker's part—as though it were a childish fantasy that could not stand up to reality.

Rick and Carl walked on, Rick sauntering a little.

Rounding the corner to the front of the building, they were alone again.

"Way to go," Carl said, putting his hand on Rick's shoulder. Rick jerked away, but Carl understood. "Man, if Wanda had been here to see that. . . ." Rick had a crush on Wanda.

Rick looked at him. "Do you think she'll hear about it?"

"Shoot, yeah."

"Did you see the way I hit him?"

"It was great." Carl felt even more elated because he knew that he was stronger than Rick. They had wrestled before. Maybe he could have vanquished the hood, too. The syllogism scarcely seemed possible.

"That stupid jerk," Rick said fiercely. "He kicked me!"

Back inside the officer's club, the lobby seemed strangely out of kilter, a dimension utterly removed from parking lots and violence. Carl felt shaky. The air-conditioned lobby with an impassive Okinawan woman standing behind a glass counter, containing candy, cigars, and antacids, was only a surface. Beneath it lay the world's seething reality of fear, violence, and pain.

CHAPTER 10

• • •

Rick stretched out as students entered the dojo. Each one bowed upon entering and headed for the dressing room. Rick went into the splits, surveying the dull wooden floor under the bare incandescent bulbs. Master Shimabatsu was not there. He often did not attend the class, delegating more and more responsibility to his assistant.

Rick turned to his right, feeling the pleasing pull on his legs, the lubrication of his hip joints. He relaxed to maximize the stretch, easing himself all the way to the floor.

He turned back to his left. A few students walked out of the dressing room, bowing again, tugging at their uniforms. They began their own warmups, gradually loosening their day-stiffened bodies.

Class would be small tonight. It was already five till seven, and only eight or nine had come in. Rick turned back to the middle and let himself down to a full split. From that position he leaned forward, spreading his arms forward like a spider hugging the floor.

When he stood, his muscles felt as if they had been poured into his skin. He snapped a couple of kicks, shook his arms out, straightened his uniform, and waited.

The last student came out of the dressing room. Rick looked at the clock. "Line up!" he said. Students jumped to their places in line. They bowed to the flag, to the instructor, and knelt on the floor for brief meditation. Then they stood up and Rick began taking them through warmups.

He paced back and forth while enumerating their situps. He did not always work out with the class. Students sweated and writhed, then at his command began leg lifts from a prone position.

Rick looked up irritably as someone appeared in the door. Being late constituted more than a minor infraction. But the man in the doorway was not a student. The slender, dark-haired American who had dropped by the day before bowed and sat on a bench to watch. Rick returned his attention to the class.

From the bench Carl watched the students go through their exercises, concentrating his attention on the teacher when the man wasn't looking in Carl's direction. Carl had waited until class began so he could observe and decide whether or not the man was Rick before approaching him. If he decided it was not Rick, he could pretend he was only watching from a sense of curiosity or nostalgia. He figured that during the course of a full class he could come to a decision.

The class itself was only mildly interesting to him. Kicks, punches, and blocks performed over and over had little appeal for Carl, which was why he had not pursued his study of the art. In his boredom he wished he could take out his knife and flip it around, but of course that would be impermissible.

The teacher seemed sensitive to his presence. Carl found little opportunity to watch him unobserved. He had hoped to be able to judge him by his voice if nothing else, but the instructor was not talkative. He barked terse commands and then enumerated the students' movements.

During the thirty-minute free period, when students worked on whatever techniques they wished, the instructor passed by Carl and nodded once. Carl nodded back. Still he could not tell.

Only when the free sparring started did Carl begin to feel sure. Almost sure. The students knelt at the edge of the tape while the teacher, his mouth chewing a rubber mouthpiece, called each one up individually for bouts of two or three minutes. Watching him move, Carl began to feel certain this was Rick.

It was not that the movements actually had anything in common with the clumsy, graceless teenager Carl had known. This black-belt athlete was amazingly fluid and balanced. But the core of his movements, the basic way his limbs were hinged to his body, the way his head moved—even the shape of the nose, the glint of the eyes—made Carl's heart throb with anticipation. Hope, which he had forced to lie dormant, began to surge in him, washing away the improbabilities.

The instructor called up a tall, blond, American student, himself a black belt, to spar. They bowed and circled each other warily. The student threw a kick to Rick's face. He was supple and fast, but Rick easily batted the kick away.

The student raised his leg to kick again, but the instructor stepped in, jammed it, and slammed a punch to the student's chest. The young man staggered back. The instructor pursued with a flurry of devastating kicks and punches. The student ducked away, panting. They faced each other, dancing lightly. The instructor moved in with a hard side kick, which the student took on his arm. The pure force of it knocked him back several feet.

The instructor attacked again. The student, apparently anticipating, spun around with a backfist. Then, at a speed so fast that only Carl's memory registered it, the instructor evaded the backfist and threw a kick to the back of his opponent's head. The kick did not seem especially hard, but the man's knees buckled as he dropped suddenly to his back, momentarily unconscious.

To Carl's surprise, no one seemed alarmed, least of all the instructor, who remained in a fighting stance. "You okay?" he asked.

"I don't know," the student managed with a half laugh. "What happened?"

"I think you turned in to my kick."

The student lay there for a moment, then got to his feet and resumed his fighting position unsteadily.

"Go real light for the next minute," the instructor cautioned. "Set your own pace."

The student nodded, and for the final minute of the fight their moves were fast but soft, with little contact. They bowed and the instructor called up another student.

Carl watched in awe. The instructor was an incredible fighter, far outclassing even the other black belts in the class. Could that funny adolescent pal of his have turned into such a man?

Carl wondered about himself. Could his own clumsy teenaged self have turned into anything deserving of respect? If this were Rick, would he have any feeling of admiration when Carl revealed his identity to him?

Carl observed the man's movements, more and more sure the instructor really was Rick Covey. It would be absurd, impossible, a miracle: Flora, and now Rick, both back here at the focal point of everything.

That's what Okinawa was, Carl suddenly realized— the focal point of his life, where his childhood had finally swung toward adolescence and manhood. This was the center, the beginning, the geographic womb. It was the only place where friendships had remained alive and vibrant in his soul, as though the island itself imbued them with an imperishable quality.

When class ended, Carl overheard the conversation between the blond student and the instructor.

"Does your head hurt?" the instructor asked with a smile.

"No. It's a funny thing. It wasn't that hard of a blow," he said, rubbing the back of his head. "It makes me think of those movies where a policeman raps a guy on the back of the head with a billy club, and he goes down. Right here at the base of the skull. What was it, your knee?"

"A kick. I saw you turn, and your head was open. I didn't think I kicked that hard, though."

"You didn't, really."

"Well, be careful. Take it easy. Don't try any complicated exercise that requires a lot of hand-eye coordination right after getting KO'd."

"All right." The student grinned. "See you, Rick."

The sound of that name made Carl quiver. Now there was no doubt. He felt as though he were floating upward like a helium balloon with its string tied to the bench where he sat. He didn't even look at Rick now. He felt etherized, as though he had witnessed the actual hand of fate moving the machinery of his life.

Rick, alone now, glanced at Carl with a frown. Carl rose. "Excuse me. Is your name Rick? Rick Covey?"

The instructor nodded suspiciously. He stared at Carl's face, seeking the hidden truth of the stranger's identity. "And you?" he asked.

A grin ruled Carl's face. In control now, he turned away slightly. He would play him. "Let's see, you lived in Okinawa when you were a teenager, right?"

Rick nodded, his frown slowly turning into a bemused grin. "Who are you?"

"Just a minute, just a minute. You'll find out who I am. You lived at Kue, not far from here. When you went into your house, there was a staircase on the right and you went up that staircase and turned right and there was your bedroom. You've got a little brother named Jim and a sister—"

"Carl? Carl Connolly?"

Carl just grinned. Rick stared at him with such intensity that Carl thought he was about to kick him. Then Rick grabbed him in a bear hug. "Carl!"

Carl hugged back.

Rick released him. "How in the . . . ? What are you . . . ? How did you find me?"

Carl waved away his questions. "Pure coincidence. I came here on vacation to visit Flora—do you remember Flora? Flora Courtier. Her name back then was Flora Anderson. She lives here and I came to visit her. We were driving around and went by Kue. I stopped to see the dojo and when I saw you, I started wondering."

"I knew there was something funny about you! I knew it."

"I wasn't sure. In fact, it didn't occur to me till that night. I woke up suddenly and thought, 'Was that Rick?' I had to come down here and see."

Rick was laughing. "When you came in tonight, I thought, 'What's that guy doing back here again?' I thought you were some kind of agent or something. You kept staring at me in class." He gripped Carl's shoulders.

"I wanted to watch you in action to make sure it was you."

"Have I really changed that much?"

"What about me? Have I?"

Rick surveyed him. "You look a little older, but you look good, strong. If I'd had any idea it might be you, I would have recognized you, but I had no idea you'd show up here."

"I know, I know. It's like me. I thought, 'Now how can that be Rick, here?' I figured it was about impossible."

"Man, it's great to see you! Let me get dressed. You don't have to go? Is there anywhere you have to be?"

"No, no."

"All right, uh, let me change, and then let's go out somewhere and eat. Have you met Master Shimabatsu?"

"Oh no, he wouldn't remember me."

"That's right, you only took a few classes. Well, come on. No, just wait here. I won't be a minute."

Rick sprinted upstairs. All the students had left the dojo. Too happy to be still, Carl drifted around the empty room, taking intense but detached interest in the old photos, the frayed flag, the floor burnished by countless bare feet, the windows that opened onto the village night.

After a while Rick appeared, looking clean and athletic in white slacks and a muscle shirt. "Hey, I don't have a car," he said, slipping his wallet into his back pocket.

"That's all right, I've got one. I'm using Flora's."

"Where do you want to go? Anywhere in particular?"

"Man, I don't know. I haven't been here in twenty years."

Rick laughed as though Carl had made a hilarious joke. "That's right, that's right. Well, I know a lot of good restaurants. Let's just go. We'll find one."

As they walked out, Carl put his hand on Rick's shoulder, squeezing the hard dome of muscle. "Man, it's good to see you."

● ● ●

They sat in the ruby glow of a Japanese restaurant. The walls were papered with glossy Oriental scenes of arched foot-bridges, tiled roofs, and gnarled trees. Carl sipped from a glass of creme de menthe on the rocks.

He had ordered it in token of the time he had gone into a bar in Koza and ordered a grasshopper—syrupy, green, and minty—and felt pleased and secretive to have gotten away with buying an alcoholic drink at the age of fourteen. Of course, back then no one paid much attention to legal age, least of all in Koza.

The place he sat now was much more placid, empty of those hordes of soldiers wearing sunshades and flowery shirts. It was a quiet restaurant, too late for a crowd.

"I won some competitions in the States," Rick said, continuing the conversation they had had in the car.

Carl sensed his friend was understating his achievements.

"I went with this girl and when it didn't pan out, I had this—I don't know—this feeling I was wasting my life. And I remembered the best times of my life, really, were in the dojo here. So I just chucked everything and came over here. Master Shimabatsu let me start back as a brown belt—"

"Even though you already had a second-degree black belt from the States?"

"I didn't tell him that. Oh no. He told me once, 'Rick, never change styles.' He wouldn't have liked to know I learned another style. He just thought I was gifted."

"Judging by what I saw tonight, you are."

Rick shook his head and gulped his ice water. "It didn't take me long to go up for black, and then second *dan*. That's all I did, all I do, is work out. He needed an assistant—he's getting old, you know—and I filled the bill."

"It sounds perfect. I never would have predicted it, though."

"I don't know if I'd call it perfect. I get bored sometimes, you know? It's like, what am I doing here? But I can't think of anywhere else I'd rather be or anything else I'd rather be doing, so I just stay here and kind of drift along."

"But you're learning more and more karate. One day you'll be a master—if you're not already."

Rick shrugged, unimpressed. "I want to hear more

about you. You were saying you write for a New Orleans newspaper? That sounds impressive."

Now Carl shrugged. "Just a staff writer. Crime beat, mostly."

"I'm not surprised you went into journalism. I remember you used to write that poetry."

"Yeah. Anyway, I worked my way up and finally landed that job in New Orleans."

"So you're on a leave of absence now? What made you come to Okinawa?"

Carl wondered how much he should tell him. He decided to hold back the bad stuff. "Flora. You never knew her very well, but she was my good friend in the ninth grade and after." It struck him as odd that he could have had two best friends who were essentially ignorant of each other.

"She your girlfriend or something?"

"Oh no. In fact, she's married. Or was. I found out when I got here her husband had just died."

"No kidding?" He frowned. "Hey, that's bad."

"I was stunned. I'd left the States before her message reached me. She's pretty depressed right now. You can believe that."

"I imagine."

"She's got two kids. Her son is in the States, senior in high school. Then there's a little girl with her here, preschool age."

"Senior in high school? She must have started young."

"Yeah, one of those early marriages. Anyway, I got here at a good time as far as helping her over her grief."

"Well, what about you? Girlfriend? Wife? What?"

Carl smiled ruefully. "Nothing. Nothing serious. What about you?"

"Looks like we're two old bachelors."

The waitress brought two handleless cups and a

sterling pot of green tea, followed by steaming plates of fried rice, and they started eating.

"I love fried rice," Carl said. "And green tea."

"I've kind of gotten used to them."

"You haven't found some Oriental beauty?" Carl asked, dipping into the rice with his chopsticks.

"I've dated some. You know. But like you said, nothing serious."

Carl nodded but felt a little uncomfortable with the subject of women, as though he and Rick were two moths circulating around the same light bulb. "What do you do when you're not teaching?"

"Nothing much." Rick grinned. "I'm sort of a barbarian. I swim, run, ride my bike, hike, work out. That's about it. Read a little. Go to church."

"Flora's a churchgoer, too. I haven't been in years."

Rick shrugged. "When are you going back to the States?"

"I don't know. I've got a thirty-day visa."

"You must be pretty high up to get an open-ended vacation."

"Yeah, well."

"And you're staying at Flora's?"

He nodded. "You'll have to come out and meet her. What are you doing tomorrow?"

Rick grimaced. "Tomorrow's Saturday. We have black-belt classes on Saturday."

"How about Sunday for dinner?"

"Sure she won't mind? Hey, you'd better check with her first, buddy."

"She won't mind. It'll help cheer her up. I'll come and get you."

"I can take a bus. Or ride my bike if it's not too far."

"No, I'll come get you. Around noon, okay?"

"Sure."

CHAPTER 11

● ● ●

When Carl got back to Flora's after eleven that night, she was sitting in the living room, reading a magazine.

"Hi," she said, almost too brightly, a handkerchief in her lap.

Emboldened perhaps by the few drinks he had had at supper, he hugged her.

She snuffled but did not cry. "That was nice," she said as he sat on the couch. "What was that for?"

"Because I'm sorry. Because I love you."

She looked away.

"Remember when I used to tell you I love you?" He felt warm and slightly off-balance from the creme de menthe. "Every time we talked on the phone. In our notes." He chuckled. "One night you told me you were going to slit your wrists and I said, 'I love you—I'll tell you a thousand times I love you,' and you giggled. Do you remember?"

She nodded.

"Then we got older and stopped saying it because . . . because it's just something you weren't supposed to say to a friend," he went on.

"I said it in my letters, even if it did make Mac mad," she said softly.

"Did it really?"

"Oh, not mad, really, but he didn't understand."

"I can appreciate that. And me, I just felt funny putting it in letters, so I quit. But I knew you knew."

"You didn't quit. Sometimes you wrote it."

"Did I?"

She nodded, smiling.

"Did you ever think I had stopped?"

She shook her head, her eyes brightly wet.

"Why not?"

She laughed. "Don't be silly."

"Well, I do love you," he declared. "I still do." He paused. "Do you ever wonder how things would have turned out if you and I had gotten married?" The question surprised even himself, as if a long-buried thought had suddenly surfaced.

"Yes," she said, nodding. "I have."

Further surprised by her answer, he said, "And?"

"And what?"

"Do you think we should have?"

She frowned. "What difference does it make now, Carl? It would never have worked out. I mean, Mac and I got married so early—I kind of got locked into a situation, you know?"

He nodded, noticing that he trembled ever so slightly. "Yeah, I know. I guess it was impossible. Still. . . ."

She looked at him sadly. "Why think things like that, Carl? Besides, we never had that kind of relationship. It's not like we didn't have a chance."

"I know. But things are different now."

"That's for sure."

"I just think—"

"Carl." She shook her head vigorously, fighting back tears. "You're forgetting—my husband just died."

He leaned forward and took her hand. "I know that, and if there were anything in the world I could do to change it I would."

"I know." She picked up her handkerchief and dabbed

her eyes. "Oh, Mac and I weren't really that much in love. Not anymore. But it's . . . after so long . . . living with somebody. . . . Still I can't—"

He nodded, feeling that he understood everything, although what he understood—the only thing he understood—was her grief, regardless of its sources. He had always understood her grief. "I wish I could do something."

"You are. Just your being here." She released his hand. "I'm just a crybaby. I'm not good for anything."

"Sure you are. Hush."

They sat quietly as she collected herself. "Well, I assume it was Rick," she said finally.

"Yes. It was great! It was really him. I invited him over for dinner Sunday. I hope that's okay."

She nodded.

"We can all go out to eat, or—"

"No, I'd like to cook something."

As he told her all about meeting Rick, she drank in his words, her eyes wide with interest, longing to be distracted from her sorrow.

When he could think of no more to tell her, he glanced around for a television listing. "What's on TV?" he asked. "Any good movies?"

"I don't know. I hardly ever watch TV."

Spotting a newspaper on a nearby chair, he grabbed it and flipped to the TV schedule. "There's a good movie on," he said. "*The Blob*. Have you seen it?"

She giggled.

"Do you have popcorn? I'll pop popcorn and we can watch a movie together."

"I'll make it."

"No you won't. Just tell me where it is."

She told him and he went into the kitchen while she turned on the TV. The movie wouldn't start for fifteen minutes. At the moment there was a rerun of "Bonanza."

As Carl shook the pot full of popping kernels on the stove, he heard Hoss and Little Joe Cartwright arguing and Ben interceding with stern wisdom.

Just as he returned to the living room with popcorn and drinks, *The Blob* came on, and they stuffed popcorn into their mouths while they watched.

Flora got tired and went to bed before the movie ended, but Carl stayed up watching Steve McQueen trying to hold off the amorphous being that threatened to consume him and all he held dear.

• • •

That night in bed Carl tossed and turned, seized by the new idea that had taken hold. Flora: He had never thought of her in that way—never. He always assumed they simply lacked the mutual chemistry that generated romantic heat. In all their teenage times together he had never felt for her anything but pure, platonic friendship.

What was different now? It had struck him when he walked in the house and saw her sitting there, vulnerable and radiant. It felt like a gradual awakening—or maybe a sudden delusion. Face it, he told himself: You're lonely, desperate, scared. She's bereaved. Don't let your weakness cloud your judgment.

Yet, she seemed so alluring to him. Wasn't it only natural now, in their adult state, that old friendship could become mutual attraction?

In the morning at the breakfast table Carl caught himself glancing at Flora when he thought she wasn't looking. She looked rumpled and sleepy in her long kimono, with no makeup, brewing coffee—but those very qualities made him wonder what it would be like if they had been married all these years.

The involuntary musings astonished even Carl. They did not arrive unaccompanied by guilt. But they stirred a longing he couldn't get rid of.

Flora sat down across from him and sipped her coffee. She seemed uncomfortable, avoiding his gaze.

"Why do you keep looking at me like that?" she said at last.

"Like what?" He hadn't realized he was that obvious.

"I don't know. Like you want to marry me or something." She giggled nervously.

The accuracy of her observation stunned him.

"I–I don't know," he said, looking down. "I didn't know I was looking at you like that."

She peered at him thoughtfully. "Carl, we're both out of sorts. This is not a normal time for us."

"No kidding." He heard Sharon's television in the background.

"Well, what's the matter then? Tell me."

He looked up. "Nothing's the matter. What do you mean, what's the matter? I didn't know I'm not supposed to look at you. Sheeee."

She frowned. "All right. Like I said, we're just out of sorts."

He forced himself to face her. "I don't know, Flora, I just wondered. . . ."

"Yes?"

"Haven't you ever wondered what it would be like if you and I . . . ?"

"You asked me that last night, Carl, and I told you. Yes, I've wondered."

"And?"

"If I remember right, that's the same thing you said last night, too. And nothing. I've wondered. I've wondered a lot of things. That doesn't mean any of them would ever happen."

"Why not?"

"You mean what if it did happen? Carl, my husband just died, for heaven's sake. He's barely cold in the ground." She bit her lip. "What do you want me to do, marry you tomorrow?"

"No. I'm sorry. I didn't mean it like that."

She collected herself. "Look, I think I know what you're feeling. Really. But now is just not the time to discuss this. Okay?"

He laughed nervously. "Okay. I apologize. I didn't mean to cause so much trouble."

"No trouble. Forget it. What do you want to do today?"

He shrugged. "Ride around. See the island. Go to a beach maybe?"

She nodded. "I know a good place up-island a little ways. There's a nice café with a beach. You can swim if you like. Sharon will love it."

"Sounds great."

"Your feelings aren't hurt, are they?"

"Of course not." He did not sound convincing.

She stood up, came around the table and hugged him. "I still feel the same way about you that I always have."

He smiled and stared at the table.

"If we're going to go, I'd better get ready," she said.

● ● ●

Sharon's blue-black hair shone in the sun, and her cheeks glowed as she dug excitedly in the sand with a yellow plastic shovel. Filling her bucket, she carried it a few steps away and dumped it.

Carl and Flora sat at a table under a big umbrella at the outdoor café. Drinking cold lemonade, they watched Sharon and the backdrop of the sea and the lava rocks that reared their heads from the shallows like sleepy, irritable sea monsters. Beyond those rocks, out past the sheltering reef, lay a small green island skirted with sandy white beach.

"I remember a place like this where I almost got sucked out into some rocks," Carl said lazily as he watched Sharon in her pink bathing suit, taking short, hurried steps to and from her pile of wet sand. "My father and I were swimming, and there was a strong outgoing tide. It started pulling me out. The thing that scared me was, I tried swimming as hard as I could toward land but I just stayed in one place. Then I noticed I was being pulled over to this big rock—kind of like that one"—he pointed—"except bigger. And there was a big whirlpool around it. I started to panic and shouted for my father. He swam out and grabbed me and we got out of the tide. But that was scary."

"Sounds like it," she said. "I was never much of a swimmer, and when I did go, it was usually at the pool at Kadena."

"Man, I used to love to snorkel. I want to do that while I'm here."

She twirled the straw in her drink, frowning at the cloudy liquid. "How long are you going to have to be in—in exile?"

"Exile?"

"In fear of your life? Running from these hit men?"

"You've been watching too many movies."

"I don't watch movies—except when you made me watch *The Blob*." Her giggle filled Carl with nostalgic affection.

"It's like I said, I'm just on vacation," he said. "If there really is a hit man, which I doubt, he's probably lost somewhere in Thailand about now. In a few days I'll call my editor and see how things stand. When they cool down, I'll go back. If they don't cool down, I'll go on somewhere else. To me, I'm not on the run, I'm having a vacation. There's a lot of places I'd like to see. And there's another advantage to all this. I'll be able to write a great series of travel articles for the paper."

She pondered this for a while. Finally she looked directly into his eyes. "Oh, Carl, you are so full of it."

Sharon ran over, the front of her bathing suit damp

and sandy, and without a word she took her mother's glass of lemonade and sucked deeply on the straw, staring at Flora's face with an intent, preoccupied expression. Finished, she set the glass down and raced back to the sand.

"I'll try not to wear out my welcome," he said. "In two weeks I'll be gone one way or another."

"You won't wear out your welcome. I don't want you to go so soon."

"Oh yes. For one thing, I imagine it will be safe for me to go back by then. It's probably safe now, but I want to take advantage of this free vacation. And two, even if they say hold off a while, I'd like to go to Japan or maybe down to Samoa."

"At least you have some idea of what you want to do."

"Still can't decide, huh?"

"I found out Mac had enough life insurance so I can go back to the States if I want and have enough to live on for a while. But—I know this seems silly—I've lived here so long it seems like home to me. On the one hand I can't bear the idea of staying by myself. On the other hand I just can't imagine leaving. You know what I'm trying to say?"

He nodded. "Yes, but I don't feel that way. I don't really feel attached to any place."

She looked at him wonderingly. "How could you not? Doesn't it make you feel sort of rootless?"

He shrugged. "I guess."

"Isn't there somebody you're attached to? Some woman or somebody?"

"Well, there's this woman where I work. But I don't know, we just . . . we're like oil and water. We like each other and we can't stand each other. I've been going around in circles with her. I think I'm better off without her."

"I'm sorry."

"Sorry? Why?"

"I just wish you could find somebody and settle down and be happy."

"Yeah, but what would that get me?"

"Peace of mind. Contentment. I don't know."

"I've never found that with any person, not in the way you mean." He looked out to Highway 1 and saw an old mama-san trudging down the side of the road with a basket full of pineapples, a scene from antiquity. "I can see how you could become attached to this place, at least the way it used to be. But it's so modernized now, it's like an American city—except for the land." He nodded to the green hills beyond the highway. "Maybe the north is still good. Sosu. But the south half, they've ruined it."

"It's not like it used to be," she agreed.

He finished his glass of lemonade, the straw gurgling in the bottom of the glass.

"How do you really feel about this—problem of yours?" Flora asked. "And I want the truth." She kicked him lightly under the table. "The truth."

He sighed. "Most of the time, or a lot of the time, I don't think about it. I think the odds are a thousand to one that the man, if there is one, is long gone. But yes, I'm afraid, or part of me is anyway. I'm on edge. I can't relax. I have a feeling for that old blues song—you ever hear of Robert Johnson?—'Hellhound on my Trail.'"

"Oh, Carl," she said in a soft voice.

"See? I knew it would upset you. That's why I didn't want to talk about it."

"I'd rather know," she insisted. "That's like me not wanting to talk about Mac, like me saying, 'Oh, I don't want to upset you.' I mean, what are friends for? What am I if you can't tell me what's really on your mind?"

"Yeah."

"I'm not some helpless little woman you have to protect from the big bad world," she said. Her indignant tone aroused in him the same feeling of nostalgia her laugh had.

"All right. I won't hide anything anymore."

"That's better. Do you want to swim?"

"Sure. Do you?"

"No, but I'll sit on the beach."

Flora sat near Sharon while Carl, who regretted his lack of snorkeling gear, swam in the clear, salty water of the East China Sea. Lying on his back on the green mattress of water, he stared at the sky, remembering how the island had looked from aboard the cargo ship *Okinawa Maru* when he and his father had gone to Japan for a vacation. The sky above the sea had been blue and uncluttered, but over the island white clouds had risen in stacks, generated by the heat and tumble of the land.

Later, tired and ready to leave, they bought an ice cream cone for Sharon and headed back south to Flora's home. The afternoon was hot, the humidity a grainy feeling in the air. Sharon complained about one thing after another on the way home.

They parked in Flora's driveway and got out. Flora fussed with her tired, grouchy daughter as they started up the walk. "You need a bath and a nap," she told her.

More whining.

Carl followed benignly.

At the door Flora put her key into the lock, turned the knob, and stopped with an air of distraction. "That's funny," she said almost to herself. "I could have sworn I locked the door when we left."

Carl felt a chill run belatedly down his spine. Flora walked in, taking Sharon straight to the bathroom. Carl examined the doorway. His stomach wrenched at the sight of scratches on the metal of the lock. Warily, he padded into the living room, eyes scanning the cool interior, hand on the butterfly knife in his pocket. Nothing appeared disturbed.

His scalp tingling, he went into his room. Everything seemed to be as he had left it. He checked the closet and under the bed. Closing his eyes, he made a deep effort to remember how he had left his belongings. He kept his passport in his suitcase in the cloth pocket along the side. He remembered that the passport had been positioned with its spine up.

With trembling fingers, he opened the suitcase. The passport was in the cloth pocket where it was supposed to be, but its spine was down. He felt the room swirl around him in a sickening revolution of chaos. He sat down on the bed and pulled out his knife, flipping it nervously as he stared into space.

● ● ●

After supper Flora tried to engage Carl in conversation, but he busied himself by flipping nervously through a magazine.

"Carl, is something bothering you?" she said at last, having set cups of hot ginseng tea on the table.

"What? No," he said, taking his drink absently.

"Are you upset about this morning?"

He frowned questioningly and blew on the hot liquid.

"You know, our talk," she clarified.

"Oh. No." He laughed slightly and glanced at the gently undulating window curtain.

"What then?"

"I'm just jumpy, that's all. Sorry." He was tempted to tell her about the apparently jimmied door, but held his tongue.

"I hope you understood what I meant," she persisted.

"What?" He frowned again, then remembered. Raw fear had displaced such leisurely thoughts as romance. "Oh—no, really, Flora. I haven't even thought about it."

"You haven't?" She chuckled, slightly confused. "That's funny. I have."

"What have you thought?" He sifted distractedly through the magazine.

"About what you said. You know—wondering."

"Really?"

"Are you listening to me, Carl Connolly?"

"Huh?" He looked up. "Sure I am."

She laughed and shook her head, then sipped her tea. "I love ginseng tea, don't you?"

"Oh, yeah. It's great."

"They say it's medicinal."

He nodded.

She peered at him. "Are you playing with me?"

He closed the magazine and set it on the table, clearing his throat. "Playing?"

"I'm trying to talk to you and you keep avoiding me."

"All right, I'm sorry. Now." He settled back and stared at her. But his gaze flickered to the window each time the curtains moved.

"I was talking about this morning. What you said," she said.

"Yes. All right. Go on."

"Well—yes, I've wondered about it."

"You mean about us?"

"Of course I mean about us! What do you think I mean?"

"And what did you conclude?"

"I didn't conclude anything, really. I've just wondered sometimes."

She nudged his knee with her stockinged foot. "I haven't ruled anything out, you know. I mean, anything's possible."

He appeared to mull over her statement.

"Not now, of course," she went on. "But it's like you said. We're adults now."

He seemed to come to himself suddenly and comprehend what she was saying.

"Really?"

"Really?" she mimicked. "Yes, really. We *are* adults now. At least I am." She giggled.

"Well, I'm sorry if I offended you this morning—so soon after the funeral and all."

She nodded. "I was a little offended, I admit. Shocked, I guess, is a better word. But I think I see what you meant."

"I apologize."

"But, well, it's like we said—we're both lonely and confused. It's only natural you would think like that."

"I guess so. I didn't mean anything by it."

"Didn't mean anything by it!" She shook her head. "Carl, sometimes I can't figure you out."

"Well, I mean, I *did* mean something by it, I guess. I just didn't intend to—shock you."

"All right, all right. I'm not shocked anymore." She drank her tea and set the cup on the table. "I just wanted you to know that—well—anything's possible, I guess."

He nodded.

"And maybe someday when all this is over and things are back to normal, well, who knows?"

He didn't know what she expected of him just now. Should he kiss her? No—that would be absolutely out of the question. He just nodded knowingly. "Good," he said.

"Anything on the movie?" she said with a grin, nodding to the television guide.

He smiled and picked it up.

● ● ●

All through church Sunday morning Carl felt sick to his stomach, his palms damp. It reminded him of the time he had gone to church after his mother's announcement of her leaving, how he had sat with Flora amid a dissolving world. But then, at least, a few milligrams of Valium had come to his rescue. That would no longer do. He wished Flora would take his hand as she had done then, but that wouldn't help either.

He was past the age of innocence, and no amount of love or medicine could protect him from the predatory menace that stalked him, fanning the yellow smoke of sickly fear within him. The preacher's words were distorted, hallucinatory. He caught fragments, and the words seemed imbued with nausea, rippling like the surface of a stagnant pool into which a pebble had been dropped. Sweat stood on his forehead as he turned the issue in his mind.

Maybe he was jumping to conclusions. The part about the position of his passport was extremely tenuous. He could have been wrong. Or maybe it had tipped over when he moved the suitcase. But the unlocked door, and the scratches on the metal . . . Well, maybe *she* left it unlocked. Maybe the scratches had already been there, perhaps from a burglary committed before he arrived, before she even moved into the house. He wanted to hurl questions at her—"Are you sure you locked it? Were those scratches there already? Has the house ever been burglarized to your knowledge?"—but he knew that would only frighten her.

The other explanation fell into place as simply as a piece of a jigsaw puzzle that has been turned over and over without fitting and finally slides in perfectly. The man had figured out Carl was on Okinawa. Using whatever information he had access to, he had learned Flora's address and broken in to seek some evidence of Carl's presence. Having found it, he had left with as little trace as possible, forgetting to lock the door. Now he would simply strike when the time was ripe.

And when would that be? As they left church? As they sat at dinner with Rick? Tonight when Carl was in bed?

Carl felt a weight of guilt. In his search for sanctuary he might have led violence straight to the heart of that which he prized most dearly, endangering the one he most would have wished to protect. He had been blind, underestimating the enemy!

But maybe he was overreacting, his nerves aggravated by anxiety. Maybe he would phone his editor. He needed advice. Should he go to the police? Leave the island immediately? Possibilities, roads lined with fear and leading to violence, channeled out from his brain inexorably. He felt trapped, unable to leave, unable to stay. A sitting duck, he could only react now, but by then it would be too late. His assassin would not be so foolish as to give him time to react.

Take Flora and run, leave the island! That was his impulse. But run where? Drag her into the horror of flight and pursuit? She would never agree to it.

Set up an ambush! But how, where, when? What if the man bided his time? Carl could not hide behind the curtains indefinitely, could not stay awake every night waiting, as he had stayed awake last night, his nerves jumping at every sound.

And all this was for what? A measly series of articles that forced one dealer out of business—as if that had in any way lessened the flow of narcotics in New Orleans. What a laugh. As soon as one steps down, two more take his place. What folly! How could he have thrown his life away on such nonsense? Just to sell newspapers? But his life wasn't thrown away yet. He'd do something. He didn't know what.

The congregation rose for the song of invitation. Carl stood, fumbling in his hymnal. Flora offered hers. "Almost persuaded now to believe, almost persuaded Christ to receive." The words flowed past Carl meaninglessly. His mouth was numb. He couldn't sing. His hands were shaking. Did Flora notice? His hand had an almost uncontrollable impulse to reach into his pocket, withdraw the butterfly knife, open the tang, turn it, flip it open, back, across, blade exposed. Up and down. Slash across. His stomach was a withered pit.

He would talk to Rick.

They sang "Blest Be the Tie." A man prayed. Then services were over, and chatter filled the sanctuary. Flora smiled and talked, introducing him to friends nearby. Carl extended a sweaty palm, examining each face for evil intent.

Outside in the blinding sunlight, he scanned the parking lot, shielding his eyes. It could come anytime. It's easy to kill a man. Just rise from behind a car—*whoosh*. With a silencer no one would even know till he fell down bleeding. Anytime, anyplace.

They got into Flora's sun-hot car. "How did you like it?" she said, oblivious to his terror.

"Fine." He stared out the window.

CHAPTER 12

● ● ●

In Kue, with Rick in the front seat beside him, Carl pulled the car over to the curb in view of Rick's old quadruplex and cut the motor. He had left Flora and Sharon at the house so Flora could cook dinner while he picked up Rick.

"Our old stomping grounds," said Rick.

"Yeah."

"Something bothering you, buddy?"

"I've got big troubles, Rick."

"Tell me about it. That's what friends are for."

"That's the same thing Flora said. Only to me friends aren't for dragging other friends into danger—real danger."

Rick waited.

"There's a contract out on me," Carl said, feeling foolishly melodramatic, as if they were two boys playing detective.

"Contract?"

"I did a series of articles on cocaine traffic in New Orleans and made the mistake of uncovering a dealer. He had to leave the country, but he put a hit man on my trail. I'm being followed."

"Why didn't you tell me about this before?"

Carl shook his head absently. "At first I thought I'd

given him the slip. We—the editors and I—planned an elaborate schedule to shake him. By the airline schedules I'm supposed to be in Thailand by now. But he must have figured it out."

"Why do you say that?"

"Someone broke into Flora's house while we were gone yesterday. She didn't even notice it, thought she'd left the door unlocked by mistake. But I saw where it was jimmied, and I found my passport tampered with."

"How so?"

"It wasn't in the same position I left it in."

"So you think this guy, this hit man, broke in to see if you were staying there?"

"Yes."

"And now that he knows, he's going to come after you?"

"You got it."

"That is bad, Carl."

Carl looked at him. Until now he had been looking away as though ashamed. "It's the worst thing that could happen. Now I've dragged Flora into this."

"I see what you mean."

"Anyway, I've got a plan. I need to know what you think. I mean, I don't know what I'm doing anymore. I need some advice."

"Shoot."

Carl laughed nervously. "That's a poor choice of words, Rick."

"Sorry."

"Well, I thought I'd book myself on a flight to Tokyo, say, tomorrow. I don't even want Flora to know about this. I'll buy the ticket and get on the plane and everything. I'll have to figure out some sort of disguise and change in the bathroom on board, then leave the plane before it takes off. Then I need to get out of Flora's house."

"You're welcome to stay with me."

"That wouldn't be any better, but thanks. What I had in mind was all of us—Flora, Sharon, you, me—taking a trip. Up north, to Sosu. I know a place. If you can. I know it's a lot to ask."

"No, no. Hey man, it's nothing. But I still don't see your plan."

"Well, if the guy gets wise and checks Flora's house, he'll see I really am gone, and he could never trace us to Sosu. I know this is stupid. I don't know anything about playing spy."

Rick laughed a little. "How will you disguise yourself?"

"I don't know. A wig? How about a Groucho Marx face, you know, the big nose and mustache and eyeglasses?" They laughed.

"I think a wig should work, and a change of clothes, maybe sunglasses," Rick said. "I'm like you, I don't know anything about this sort of thing."

"The thing is, it could all be my imagination. I mean, I can't be sure my passport was moved. And maybe she really did leave the door unlocked."

"No, I think you should assume the worst. That way you can't go wrong."

"That's what I thought."

"What's at Sosu?"

"It's a place, just a big cliff where we used to go for church camp at the north end of the island. Actually Sosu is a village, but the camp is about half a mile or so from there. Very isolated, beautiful."

"Why do you need me? I mean, I'll be glad to go, but . . ."

"Moral support, I guess. I don't know. If things get bad I guess I need somebody I can rely on."

Rick nodded. "Taking off should be no problem. I haven't taken any time off in a year. I'll just tell Master Shimabatsu I have to be gone for a week, and either he can teach or get someone else to fill in."

"Can you get hold of a couple of tents?"

"I can try."

"I'll call the airport this afternoon after dinner and try to book a flight for tomorrow. I'll figure out all the details later. I'm scared to death, man. I don't mind telling you."

"I don't blame you."

"Do you think all this will work? I can't find any flaw with it."

"It sounds all right to me." But doubt edged Rick's voice.

"If I can just make him think I've left Okinawa, then Flora will be safe. After that I really will leave, and then I can deal with whatever comes up. I just can't stand the thought of getting her into all this."

"I know what you mean."

Carl cranked the ignition. "Things are a lot different now than they used to be, aren't they?" he said bitterly. The sight of his old neighborhood aroused no nostalgia in him now. The present weighed too heavily on him.

"Well, buddy," Rick said, punching Carl's arm lightly, "it's nothing we can't handle."

Carl managed a smile, feeling a hint of hope. Then he drove out into the street to face the blinding uncertainty of the future.

● ● ●

Of course, Carl wound up telling Flora the whole plan. He simply could not lie to her. Besides, he couldn't pull off the scheme without arousing her suspicion. How could he carry luggage and take a cab to Naha without her asking questions? And he remembered her remark about not being a little woman he needed to protect.

Dinner over, they sat in the living room drinking coffee while Sharon played outside. Rick and Flora had hit it off well, easily bridging the gaps in conversation left by Carl's preoccupation.

As they sipped their coffee, Carl told Flora the entire scenario—from her finding the door unlocked to his faking a departure to Tokyo to their all going to Sosu. Flora paled with fear when Carl told her of the suspected break-in, but as he outlined his plan, her cheeks flushed with excitement. Rick sat silently impassive, a tanned Viking inured to danger.

"We'll need to leave Tuesday morning, then," Flora said. "No, Monday afternoon, as soon as you get back."

Carl nodded. "We don't want to give him any chance of seeing me here."

The "him" they spoke of had now assumed a definite identity. In Carl's mind he was some ghetto meathead, cunning enough to track him and single-minded as a bulldog. He saw primate features, a determined scowl, seedy clothes, a hand reaching for his armpit holster. He saw a man irritated at the hassles of overseas travel but uncannily patient, the price high enough to make him endure the insults of customs guards and the complexities of foreign cultures.

Carl simply hoped there was only one, a him and not a them. Or better yet—but this was too much to hope— that there was no one, that it was all the figment of a frightened imagination, or that if there had ever been a hit man, he had given up long since.

"I think the Sosu trip is a wonderful idea, Carl," Flora said.

Carl smiled. Far from feeling jealous, he liked the lively, almost flirtatious way Flora had acted around Rick during dinner. It was her normal way of acting with men, especially handsome men, and Carl hoped it indicated a lessening of her widow's grief.

"How did you think of it?" she asked.

He laughed ruefully. "I stayed awake all Saturday

night. I couldn't sleep after the break-in. I thought and thought and that was what I came up with."

"Well, Sosu sounds great." Her cheerfulness was almost contagious. "We won't have to be worrying about the bogeyman, and it sounds like a great place for a vacation. Sharon ought to love it."

Rick agreed. "I'll try to get the tents in the morning."

"Yeah, we'll need to make a list," Flora said.

"Snorkeling gear," said Carl. "The snorkeling up there is great."

"I've got some gear," Rick said.

"We've got some, too, somewhere," Flora said. "Mac and I tried it a time or two."

"It's really fabulous," Carl said, conscious of the deadliness underlying these summer vacation plans, like rumors of a psychopath at a Girl Scout camp. "There's a stream that comes out of the mountains, and a really neat pool we can swim in, too, with a little waterfall."

"I can use a trip like this," Rick said. "I haven't done anything out of my ordinary routine in a long time."

"We can stay a few days, play it by ear," Carl said. "Afterward, when the coast is clear, I can go on to Samoa or somewhere."

"Don't talk about that," Flora said, reaching out to squeeze his arm. "We like having you here. Don't we, Rick?"

Rick laughed. "It's almost as good as reading a spy novel."

CHAPTER 13

• • •

That night, at Carl's suggestion, they all went out, leaving Sharon at a baby-sitter's. Carl did not want to stay around the house, where he felt like a target. He wanted to make things as safe as possible until they could get away up-island.

At a restaurant in Koza Carl drank saki while Rick and Flora drank tea. He drank liberally to drown out his anxiety.

"It's funny, Rick," said Flora. "When Carl first mentioned you to me, I didn't remember you at all. But now it's coming back." She closed her eyes, summoning a mental picture. "You had short brown hair with a little curl right in front—yes, I remember. I thought you were cute."

"He had a crush on Wanda Walsh," Carl said. "You remember Wanda, Rick? With the beautiful arms?"

Rick laughed and took refuge in his teacup.

Flora looked at them with amusement. "What beautiful arms?"

"Did you know Wanda Walsh? She was in Rick's and my homeroom," Carl explained. "Rick thought she had beautiful arms. I don't know, her arms looked normal to me."

"Aw, how cute," Flora teased. "A romantic. That must be why you and Carl were good friends."

Her words warmed Carl with nostalgia. He looked at Flora, and she seemed to glow—as beautiful as ever, her eyes rich and dark and lively. Despite the storms she had weathered, she had scarcely changed. She was still as he remembered her.

Rick was the surprise. From the gawky boy of high school days he had become an eagle of a man—strong, powerful, perceptive—in a way that Carl never could have predicted.

"Flora had a crush on J.T.," Carl told Rick. "Remember J.T. Carr? Actually, J.T. was the one who had a crush on her. She just strung him along."

"Carl! I never strung anybody along." She laughed.

"She left a trail of broken hearts at Kubasaki."

Rick was grinning. "Yeah, it's funny. I remember you, Flora, but I didn't realize you two were such good friends. I thought Carl had a crush on you but just didn't admit it."

Flora and Carl exchanged secret smiles, and Flora said, "He probably did, poor thing."

"No, I had a crush on Rosette. I almost got her to like me, too."

"You scared her away," Flora said. She turned to Rick. "I had it all lined up. I'd told Rosette what a great guy Carl was—boy, did I have to do some exaggerating—no, I'm kidding—and she was all excited about him. And then I don't know what he did, but he scared her off."

"I wrote on her doll," Carl said.

"What?"

He smiled sheepishly. "Her mother gave her one of those big animal dolls people are supposed to autograph. Well, I used to joke around, saying, 'Rosette is dumb,' so I wrote in big—I mean *big*—letters, 'Rosette is dumb.' It covered one whole side."

"Carl!" Flora said in mock horror. "No wonder she stopped liking you."

Rick swirled a spoon in his teacup. "I was so bashful around girls I could hardly speak to one if I liked her."

Flora peered at him. "I can see why people think you're bashful. I don't think you are, though."

"I'm not anymore, but then I was terrified."

"It's true. He was," Carl said. "But so was just about everybody—the boys, anyway."

"What a crazy time of life," Flora said. "And do you believe—this is really incredible—do you believe I now have a son who is a senior in high school?"

The waitress brought their food, and Carl ordered another glass of saki.

"Doesn't it make you feel horribly old?" Flora continued as they ate. "It probably doesn't affect you two like that, but it does me."

"Well," Rick said, "I'm maybe not as quick or strong as I was when I used to compete. I'm past my fighting prime, I suppose. But I feel like I can still outfight most of the kids. Maybe not in the ring, but if it were a matter of life or death . . . I feel like I'm smarter, more cunning than I used to be. They may have faster and fancier kicks, but it's more important to know how to lay back and then strike with just that one deadly strike, the one that counts."

Carl and Flora stared at him as though he were speaking in allegory.

Flora laughed sadly. "I've had a husband and two children. Sometimes that weighs on you, makes you feel old."

"But not all the time," Carl said.

"No, not all the time. But I've lost something since those years in high school. Maybe we all have, or maybe it's just me. Something just goes away and doesn't come back."

"Yeah, but to me it seems like it never dies," Carl said.

"It's like there's a world where all those things happened and maybe are still happening."

Flora smiled. "There's a house in Kansas where my grandparents lived when they were alive. I remember seeing a picture of them when they were young and thinking somehow they're still like that—somewhere, maybe in that house, in another dimension—still young and happy and in love."

Rick motioned to the waitress for more water.

Carl sensed his old friend had little capacity for the sacredness of nostalgia. He looked at Flora and wondered what flame had gone out of her. It disturbed him to think that she might not be the happy, full-of-life girl he had known back then, that she might be a flower in the process of wilting and fading. How could it be? Such a crime, such a sin.

"I remember how dramatic everything seemed back then," he said. "Every emotion!"

"Yes," Flora replied.

"We can laugh now only because we have the perspective of distance. I think everything we felt then was real, just as real to us then as what we feel now."

Flora nodded. "Me too." She gazed at Carl, then looked down.

Rick shrugged. "I don't know. In a way my prime is past, but in a way I'll never reach my prime. I'll always strive toward it . . ." His words trailed off, somehow suggestive of the mysteries of the martial arts. "But sometimes I feel like I'm stagnating. It's like I'm not getting anywhere. I used to think it was my purpose to be a famous tournament champion, but somehow that doesn't seem too important anymore. I believe God has given me a purpose, but what?" He shrugged again.

After they finished eating, they went outside. Koza on a Sunday night was not especially busy. Rounding the corner of the restaurant to the small, dark parking lot, they passed a large garbage bin, deep in night shadow.

Carl heard a voice, a hissing sound. He turned and saw three men standing in the shadow. One held something that looked like a knife.

"Pretty lady," one of them said. The other two laughed gutturally.

Even Rick, with reflexes honed to incredible speed, was surprised at Carl's action.

Without hesitation, without time to surmise or observe, Carl whipped the butterfly knife from his pocket, opening it in the same fluid motion, and sprang at the knife-wielder. His left hand grabbed the man's wrist and jerked it aside while his right hand came across in a short arc and laid the stainless steel edge of his knife blade to the man's throat. Carl backed him to the wall.

The other two men, utterly unprepared for the attack, fled. The single thug was left helpless against the wall, unable even to speak from the pressure of the blade at his throat.

"Carl!" Flora gasped.

Rick stepped forward. "Wait," he told his friend. "Don't."

Only something thin and intangible kept the knife from cutting into the throat, laying the man's neck open. Rick reached out and took the knife from the hoodlum's all-too-willing hand.

"I've got his knife, Carl," Rick said gently, persuasively. "Now let him go."

Carl did not move. He was frozen, locked in indecision, a prisoner of his knife's intent. Rick placed his hand on Carl's shoulder and gently pulled him back. Carl yielded.

When he stepped back, trembling fiercely, they saw that the man was just a boy, a teenaged hoodlum hoping to scare some restaurant-goers out of a few yen. His eyes wide with fear, his trousers newly stained, he shook like a rabbit.

"It's all right," Rick said to Carl. "He's nothing. Let him go."

Still Carl did not move.

The youth remained motionless, apparently afraid Carl would spring again.

"Carl," Rick said again. "It's not *him*. It's just a boy. I've got his knife. Let him go."

"Better yet, turn him over to the police," Flora said.

"All right," Rick conceded. "The police." He had not thought of that. He had sought only to deter violence.

Flora went back into the restaurant and came out with several men. Shortly afterward the police arrived, and the boy was bundled into the police car and taken away.

The restaurant manager apologized profusely, offered to reimburse them for their meal, and invited them back anytime for a free supper.

Flora and Rick tried to shake Carl out of his murderous daze. They could not make him put away his knife, but they got him into the back seat of Flora's car. As they drove away, they heard the rhythmic click-click of the flipping butterfly knife.

CHAPTER 14

• • •

After Flora went to bed, Carl got up and propped a chair against the front door. That was probably stupid. The man could come in just as easily through a window. But since he came in through the door last time—well, it made Carl feel better to take the precaution.

He returned to bed, lights off, and listened to the night sounds. How many more nights could he live with this fear? It was eating him up inside like a cancer, establishing its own domain to which he must pay fealty.

Three weeks had come and gone since this fear entered his heart, since the word was passed to him that his life wasn't worth betting on. Terror had hit him then. Actually, it was more like an awakening, a serious understanding that he could be killed, and had grown into a steady hum of anxiety and watchfulness, light sleeping and edginess.

It struck him hard in Mexico City. In a tawdry hotel with bad plumbing and abundant cockroaches, suspicious characters everywhere and his intestines burning up with the runs, he felt his life turn inside out like a hideous rubber Halloween mask—pinkly naked with fleshy wrinkles.

He had sat on his bed, hunched over with searing guts, listening to the growls of traffic, smelling the smog, watching a giant cockroach sneak behind a dresser where it waited with uncanny patience for him to stop looking. It would be the worst thing in the world for his life to end here.

He had rushed to the bathroom, eyes watering with pain, thinking: Now, now would be the worst time. Now the door could open, and the man could come in and calmly do it. He felt like a spider being washed down a drain.

Finally he dragged himself to his lumpy bed and lay there, hot despite the pathetic air conditioner, listening to the alien noises, his heart having sunk and merged into an amorphous mass of fear in his guts.

He went back to the bathroom and vomited. Maybe he had a fever. Once upon a time there was a mother who held a damp washrag to his head when he was sick. Who could comfort him now?

Back on the bed, he longed to call Sally, his lady friend at the newspaper. No matter that they were on the outs, she was someone. Maybe he could milk from her dry soul a few drops of compassion. He picked up the phone, asked the hotel operator to put in the call, then hung up and waited.

Long moments passed. He began to feel foolish. The phone rang and he picked it up.

"We are putting your call through now," the operator said.

He heard the tinny sound of a phone ringing hundreds of miles away, then a rasping like a tubercular cough, a sizzling like frying bacon. There came a thin "Hello?" at the bottom of a deep well.

"Hey, Sally," he said.

"Hello?"

"Sally!" he shouted. "It's me. Carl. Carl Connolly."

"What? Hello!"

"Carl! Carl Connolly!"

"He's not here."

He remembered the old Abbott and Costello shows. They could have used this routine.

"It's after midnight," Sally's voice said. "Who is this?"

After midnight? He stepped to the bathroom, dragging the phone with him, and looked at his watch. It was indeed after midnight.

"Hey," he said. "This is Carl!"

"Carl? What do you want?" She sounded cross.

How could he answer her? What did he want? "I just wanted to talk," he said at last.

"What? I can't hear you."

"Talk!" he said angrily. "I just wanted to talk!"

"Oh."

Bending slightly from the stomach cramps, he tried to think of something to say. Finally he said, "Bad connection. I'll call back later." He hung up.

He fell asleep around three and woke at six, moments before his wake-up call.

His fear traveled with him. All those nebulous ports of entry and exit, the lizard-faced customs officers, the sickening clusters of creatures who were his fellow humans. He carried the fear and it became a cold, hard nugget in his body. By the time he arrived in Okinawa, it was at least down to manageable size.

But after the break-in it had ruptured like a cocoon, and a great, luminous moth of terror began to beat against the walls of his chest, trying to get out. He tried to sleep, wishing those wings would tire. He imagined himself as that moth, captured in a clammy dungeon. He folded his wings together, resting, but kept his antennae erect, alert. That was how he slept.

● ● ●

Up-island, Carl got off the bus at the open-air café where he and Flora had taken Sharon on Saturday. He felt ludicrous in his ill-fitting brown wig and heavy black-lens sunglasses. Hoping no one would detect his disguise, he sat down at a table, ordered coffee, and lit his pipe. He glanced out to the beach, deserted, pristine.

The airport charade had gone off without a hitch, but it seemed so ridiculous that Carl had the feeling he was out of sync with reality. Perhaps there was no assassin at all, just his excited imagination and a few random circumstances thrown together to keep him agitated.

He had bought the ticket and gone on board, carrying a small suitcase. Although he glanced around at the crowd in hopes of spotting his would-be stalker, he was afraid to be too obvious. As soon as he boarded the plane, he went straight to the bathroom, quickly changing clothes and donning his wig and glasses. He came out, put the suitcase above the nearest seat, then left the plane, telling the stewardess he would be back in a second.

Once back in the airport he felt both free and fearful. What if the stalker detected the ruse before the plane left? Carl left the airport quickly, not waiting to find out. Boarding a northbound bus, he rode it through Naha, up Highway 1—the bus stopping constantly to take on or let off passengers—and finally past Kadena Circle till he saw the café.

The plan seemed foolproof. He had left all traces of himself behind on the plane. There was no way he could be traced now. There had not even been an American on the northbound bus. In a while Flora, Sharon, and Rick would arrive in Flora's car, he would get in, and they would all vanish to the nooks and crannies of the island's northern end, untraceable.

Still, he had the nagging feeling he was making much ado about nothing. Well, better too right than too wrong. A mistake in this game could be deadly. Perhaps it was his present security that made him survey his past fears with such doubtfulness. It seemed unlikely an assassin would trail him around the world like this. The man he had exposed had not been that powerful or vengeful, surely. The bounty would have to be hefty to take care of all the plane fares.

He was probably forgotten once he left New Orleans, he reflected as he drank the coffee. That made sense. A hit man was prepared to gun him down in New Orleans, but certainly not to follow him to the ends of the earth.

Death threats weren't uncommon anyway. Every cop who put away a crook was threatened. Every convicted dope criminal vowed vengeance. It rarely came to anything. Quite possibly Carl was making a royal fool of himself, dressing up in a wig and playing the spy. He had half a notion to pull off the wig now and resume a normal, carefree life. But the thought of Flora and Sharon stopped him. The slightest possibility that they could be hurt mandated utter caution.

He looked across Highway 1 to the rocky green slopes. The thought of those hills stretching away to the north stirred him. Soon he would be getting into country he had not seen since boyhood, when he had gone there for church camp. The winding highway led between mountains on one side, sea on the other. He remembered the view from the cliff at Sosu, a curtain of gray rain trailing over the sea, back and forth, indecisive. The nights with a million stars. He closed his eyes.

Flora's car crunched on the gravel of the parking lot. Carl downed his coffee and walked over. Flora's smiling face looked up at him. Happiness seemed to exude from the car. Rick sat in the passenger's seat, and Sharon cheerfully leaned forward between the bucket seats.

"Going my way?" Carl asked.

"Sorry, we don't give rides to strangers."

Carl grinned through his disguise, and Sharon let out a giggle as he climbed into the back seat with her.

"How'd it go, buddy?" Rick said, turning with his arm on the back of the seat. His imposing physical presence was a comfort to Carl, shedding an aura of warm strength and security. If Carl was like an erratic viper with his knife, Rick was a confident, unperturbed tiger, rested and fed and afraid of nothing.

"Great." Carl smiled at Sharon, who watched wide-eyed as he took off the wig and glasses. Smoothing his mussed hair with his palm, he eyed himself in the rearview mirror, glimpsing Flora's intent face as she drove them up Highway 1.

"See anybody that looked suspicious?" Rick asked.

Carl shook his head. "To tell the truth, I felt kind of like that inspector—what's his name?—you know, from the Pink Panther movies?"

Flora laughed abruptly.

"Pink Panther!" Sharon exclaimed in delight.

Carl tousled her pretty black hair. "Yeah, Pink Panther," he growled playfully.

She giggled again.

"You seem like a cheerful bunch. What's been happening?"

"You should have seen us packing," Flora said. "It was worse than any Girl Scout trip I've ever been on. Carl, we couldn't find anything. We were going in circles."

"We really were," Rick said.

"I must have had to go to the store ten times. We're the most disorganized campers in the world!"

"Mommy forgot the toilet paper," Sharon said.

Flora giggled uncontrollably. "Carl, why didn't you tell us all this was involved? I'd forgotten how much junk you need for a simple camping trip."

"I can't even remember the last time I went," Rick said.

"I hate to put you to all this trouble," Carl apologized.

"Oh no, it's been a blast," Flora said with a laugh. "We're just so disorganized."

"Then we started talking about Kubasaki," Rick prompted.

"Yeah, the ol' alma mater," she said, struggling to suppress her laughter. She had not laughed that much since Carl had come. "We knew a lot of the same people, even if we didn't really know each other well. Mr. Shuffway—remember him?"

"Latin teacher?"

"Yes. Oh Carl, remember how he would say,"—she pursed her lips—" 'Now class, I want you to conjugate *agricola*'?"

"Really?" Carl frowned. "Conjugate *agricola*? I thought you only conjugated verbs."

"See what good we got out of Latin? 'Conjugate *agricola*,'" she mimicked.

"I showed him my poetry one time," Carl said. "He didn't like it. I don't think he liked any poetry after Homer or Virgil."

"Virgil?" Flora cackled again. "Do you remember Virgil? Glasses, big feet, terrible complexion?"

Rick turned to Carl. "Didn't we have him in P.E.?"

"No," Carl said, catching Flora's giddiness. "That was somebody else. I know who you're talking about. Virgil was this real creepy-looking guy."

"Oh yeah, I remember him. What a dope—"

"Just a minute, fellows," Flora said reprovingly. "We're kind of sinking back to the level of junior high kids, aren't we? I mean, aren't we getting a tad cruel?"

"You're right," Rick said.

"I'm sorry, Flora," Carl said. "Anyway, I had this good friend for a while named Lou. He was into sniffing glue."

"Hey, that rhymes," Flora said.

"Talk about junior-high mentality," Carl chided.

"All right, all right," Flora conceded.

"There were some real hard guys at K-9," Rick said. "I mean, the kind you wouldn't want to mess with. I wonder whatever became of them."

"They're probably sitting around with a bunch of kids

and a beer gut, watching TV," Flora said. A shadow seemed to fall over her, but she shook it off.

"Or in prison," Carl said.

"Do you remember Gwinn? He was a real hood," Rick said.

"I knew him," Flora said. "He was a nice guy."

"Listen to her," Carl said. "Sure, they're nice guys when you're a pretty girl. When you're a guy it's different."

"Well, you two have turned into a couple of hard guys, it seems to me. Rick here is an nth degree black belt in karate, and you're a knife-fighting expert."

"Yeah, but we're not tough," Carl said. "At least, I'm not. I imagine Rick is. Being tough—I don't know, it takes something I don't have."

"You looked pretty tough in the parking lot last night," Flora said.

"Yes, but he's right," Rick agreed. "Some guys are just naturally tough, know what I mean? They're not necessarily good fighters. They just keep coming."

"People used to think Mac was a hard guy, but I never thought of him that way," Flora said. "He was real sweet back then."

"Women and men must inhabit different worlds. Did you know Mac?" Carl asked Rick.

"Did he have longish hair and play on the football team?"

"Yes."

"I saw him around. I didn't really know him."

"Mommy, I've got to use the bathroom," Sharon called.

"Oh, we should have stopped at that café. I didn't think about it," Flora said. "We'll stop at the next place, honey."

They stopped at the next gas station, which had the ocean for a backyard, and Carl bought everyone snacks and soft drinks. For the first time his worries began to feel far, far away.

CHAPTER 15

• • •

Flora sat in the back seat with Sharon's head in her lap while Rick drove. From the passenger seat in front, Carl watched the rice paddies and hills in the well-populated stretch north of Nago. Elderly farmers wearing wide cone-shaped straw hats pushed wheelbarrows full of manure.

There were water buffalo grazing, fleets of boys on bicycles, clusters of girls walking along holding hands, ancient crones at pineapple stands. The air smelled rich with vegetation and woodsmoke.

Carl noticed Flora's eyelids drooping while Rick held the wheel with an impassive stare. Carl settled back in his seat, tired from lack of sleep and the strain on his nerves, watching the countryside pass in a blur. The rocks that came down into the sea in the exact shape of a brontosaurus. The waterfall that tumbled from high up the mountain.

He remembered an old road sign: Plenty Carves at Forwoad, an Okinawan attempt at English, meaning "curves ahead." He wondered when the memories would merge with reality and all would be whole or dead or reborn.

Carl thought wistfully of Sally in New Orleans. The trouble was, she was so good-looking—golden-brown hair streaked with blond, golden tanned skin, eyes that could be so penetrating and inviting and could close up petulantly. He and she had been hopelessly paired, utterly incompatible. Her childish philosophy—she was several years younger, after all—was to live for the moment, spurn serious thinking, and just have fun. Why trouble with gloomy thoughts and memories and questions?

When he was with her, watching her prance out of the water in her glossy one-piece clinging bathing suit, Carl fell in line with her philosophy: yes, sensuality, forgetfulness, immersion in pleasure. But that had to pall. He couldn't maintain that twenty-four hours a day, try as he might. It was too innocuous. And her friends! What dolts.

He had become impatient and irritable, wanting to get her away by herself to talk, but she just said, "Oh, Carl! Why are you always so serious?" Better, thought she, to party and laugh at stupid jokes and see forgettable movies than to sit quietly in an apartment, listening to soothing music and talking, just talking. For Sally there could be no gaps for reflection, for pausing and looking and contemplating. Just move, like a shark.

They went back and forth, each admiring something in the other but unable actually to accept that something, the whole misbegotten affair spurred on by mutual physical attraction—and then the job, having to work together. But just now he forgot all that, that abrasive feeling she caused in him as her laughter scraped against his heart. He wished she were here with him for the physical comfort, the warm presence she had, the silent burying of one another, the hand in hand and the electricity that sparked there.

Yes, they had their good moments. They had met sometimes like two trapeze artists for a brief moment in midair. The rest of the time they were either swinging toward or away from one another.

Watching Okinawa blur past in the afternoon drizzle, hot and humid and pungent, he wished Sally were here and they could stop and drink cold beer and, yes, live for the moment. If he could just hold her and steal the comfort she held, he would pretend to have fun. He could do with the island of her golden flesh now. He could stand living for the moment for a while. He'd had a glut lately of past and future, of deep thoughts and unanswerable questions and the gaping darkness that seemed to underlie his footing.

He wondered, did she miss him? Was she worried about him? Or was she too busy partying, had she taken up with someone else and forgotten him entirely, consigning him to a past not worth remembering? He sighed and felt miserable and hollow. He needed rest. His nerves were frayed from his too-long flight, from the constant restlessness that gnawed inside him.

Now, at last, he felt truly free of his shadowy stalker, invulnerable, invisible. He had given him the ultimate slip. What he would do after Sosu Carl didn't know, but it wouldn't matter. Even if the man figured out the ruse and returned to Okinawa, it would be too late to find him. After Sosu, maybe, Carl would put on his disguise and go somewhere else. He would call his editor and ask for advice. Maybe there was news. Maybe the coast was clear and he could come back and resume his life.

It was wonderful to be with Rick and Flora, but he was ready to get on with living. Okinawa, for all its nostalgia, had changed and aged just as he had. Time had not stopped here or anywhere else.

In a way he had hoped to find his memories here intact as he had left them, as if at Kue he could have seen himself, young Carl, playing basketball with Rick, as if he could have driven out to Kubasaki—was it still standing?—and seen Flora and himself standing outside after play practice, or climbed the stairs of his old home and picked up the phone and called Flora—the girl

Flora—talking until ten, then hanging up and talking again secretly at ten-thirty.

But all that was gone. Okinawa was a different place. How did time perform this magical disappearing act?

Oh, Sally, let's have a drink and go to bed. Let the party begin, or end. Carl fell asleep, his head resting between the door and the back of his seat.

When he woke, cotton-mouthed, Rick was driving with the same steady stare. "Want me to drive?" Carl offered.

"I don't mind."

"Why don't you let me? I'm awake."

"All right." Rick pulled over.

"What is it?" Flora asked sleepily from the back.

"Nothing," Rick said. "Switching drivers."

Carl got behind the wheel and they started off again. They had come a long way since Nago. Little traffic traveled Highway 1 now as it followed the craggy coastline.

Carl felt refreshed by his sleep. The overcast yielded no rain, but the air was clean and cool, sweet with the smell of sea and hills. The little car hugged the road, responding well. He poured himself a cup of coffee from a thermos that lay between the two bucket seats. Though not steaming, it was still warm.

"How long has it been since you've been up this far?" Carl asked Rick in a low voice. He didn't want to disturb Flora and Sharon.

"To tell you the truth, it's been years. I don't travel very far from Jagaru. The farthest I go is a beach where I snorkel, above Bolo Point."

"Did you bring snorkeling gear?"

"You bet, buddy."

"Good. It's been years since I've snorkeled."

"We'll go out. It's one of my favorite things to do. I'll bet the snorkeling's great up here."

"It is. Man, it is. Did you have trouble getting all the camping gear?"

"Not really. Our main trouble was getting organized. I got two tents, a big one for them and a two-man for us. Borrowed them from a friend. We've got enough food for several days."

"There's a little store in the village of Sosu where we can buy stuff if we need it."

"We've got a camp stove and an ice chest. Plenty of drinks."

"I think they have a faucet up there—I mean, assuming it's all as I remember and that no one cares if we camp there. It used to be a church camp, and our group came up here once or twice a year. There's a little concrete building for a kitchen and a covered pavilion for an eating area and that's all. We used to bring army tents."

"Sounds great."

"Even if there's somebody there, I'll just explain that I used to go to the church and wanted to camp."

"Hope they haven't sold it."

"Hey, as far as I'm concerned my worries are behind me. None of these little worries matter, know what I mean?" A feeling of exhilaration swept over him. "Who cares? We're free. Besides, there are a million places to camp up here. Miles of beach. We don't even need to go to that spot."

"Great."

"Why don't you nap?"

"I think I will."

CHAPTER 16

● ● ●

At Hedo Point they stopped to stretch their legs and eat. As Flora and Rick spread food and drinks out on a picnic table, Carl took Sharon's hand and led her to a waist-high concrete fence at the cliff's edge. He picked her up and set her on top of the fence, gripping her by the waist, and let her look over. A stiff wind blew off the ocean.

After one glimpse, Sharon squirmed. "I'm scared. I want down." She ran back over to the picnic table.

Carl sat on the fence and looked down. He didn't know how far this cliff plunged straight down, but he would have guessed five hundred feet, maybe a thousand. It was a long, long drop to the shallows below, a good place for hara-kiri. He wondered how many had been committed here during World War II. From here Carl had an eagle's-eye view into the crystalline seawater below. Past the reef's bony rim it dropped off to deep blue, seemingly bottomless.

"Food's ready," Flora called.

"Come look at this," Carl replied.

Rick came over with Flora, who was tugging at Sharon, and the three adults peered into the abyss.

Flora didn't look long. "Ugh, that makes me dizzy." She turned away, to Sharon's obvious relief.

"Long drop," Rick said.

Overhead the afternoon sun was a brassy ball, and the gusting wind was cleansed by untold miles of salt water and globe circling.

"How much farther?" Flora asked Carl as they gathered around the table to eat.

"I'm not sure."

Weariness showed on them all.

"Oh, I forgot to give you something." Flora rummaged in her purse and took out an envelope. "It was addressed to me, so I opened it, naturally. I didn't read it, though."

Carl recognized Sally's handwriting. That was smart of her, not putting his name on the envelope. An unnecessary precaution, no doubt. Carl had trouble believing some petty hit man had inside access to the U.S. mail. Sally must have gotten Flora's address from Carl's editors.

Carl ate quickly and left the table to sit on the fence.

"Dear Carl," Sally's zany scrawl began.

You'd think she would have used a typewriter, he thought.

I'm sorry we weren't able to talk on the phone. Your call woke me, and I really had trouble figuring out what was going on. Plus I couldn't understand half of what you were saying. Anyway, I'm sorry. I know you probably felt like talking to someone and have no doubt had a hard time on your trip.

Ed says nothing's new and you might as well count on staying in the saddle for a few weeks anyway. That's what he said, "in the saddle." At least you're getting to see some exciting places—though not in the best of circumstances.

Things are the same as always around the office. Your duties have been shared, but mainly Paul is covering your beat. He's glad to get the overtime, but you know how uptight they get about overtime. They're talking about hiring somebody temporary, but that's another keg of worms.

I'm very busy. The usual stuff. Well, take care.

Your friend,
Sally

He read it through again, searching for even a hint of affection. The emotional barrenness of the letter left him feeling empty. Yes, it was as he had predicted. She had more or less forgotten him. They probably told her to write the letter for the sake of his morale. Great. A real morale booster. "Your friend, Sally."

Thanks, friend. Not a thing. Not even "I hope you're all right" or "Are you feeling okay?" or "I miss you" or "I've been thinking about you." Just "sorry the phone call didn't go well"—sorry on his account, moreover, since he needed to talk, not she. Then nothing but office gossip. So Paul's getting overtime. Great. Carl's been trying to bypass the River Styx and Paul's glad to get overtime.

Carl crumpled the letter and envelope into a tight ball and threw it hard out over the cliff. Instead of the wad wafting down to become a speck on the water, a gust of wind caught it and pushed it back against the cliff, lodging it among the sharp lava rock and prickle-leafed bushes. Let the ants eat it, he thought.

Rick and Flora had put everything away and were sitting at the empty table across from each other, talking intently while Sharon played nearby. Watching them unnoticed, Carl was surprised by the intensity between them, a beam of eye contact uniting them. He walked over and Flora looked up. "News from home?"

"Sort of. Nothing important."

"Oh. Well, ready to go?"

"Yeah."

Carl sat in the front to give Flora directions while Rick sat in back with Sharon. They passed through the knotted hills on the north end of the island and swung around to a flat stretch with open sandy beach to their left, where the open Pacific merged with the East China Sea. "We're turning back to the south," Carl noted. "Hedo's the northernmost point, then we go back south a little ways to Sosu, on the Pacific side."

The road curved along the edge of the hills, the sea always on their left but to the east now, and Carl tingled with excitement as they plunged deeper into this remote sanctuary of mountains and bush, Okinawa's last holdout. One day, probably soon, this would become a place of villas and golf links. The developers would get to it: Sosu Estates.

His eyes scanned the surroundings hungrily as they drove. The farther they went, the better he felt. He was becoming free: free of his stalker, free of Sally, free of worries. He and his companions would bury themselves in these hills. Maybe he would send them back and remain up here—a hermit, beach bum, adopted villager—find a little patch of ground, raise a garden, build a thatched hut, fish in the sea, roam the hills.

He leaned forward. "That's it."

Flora slowed. "Where?"

"No, I mean that's the stream. Look." They passed over a bridge. Underneath, a shallow, clear stream flowed out of the hills into the sea. On their left it fanned out and the clear fresh water merged with the salty, a zone of compromise. "If you take a trail up here and follow this stream, you come to that swimming hole I was telling you about, the one with the waterfall."

"Waterfall?" Sharon echoed. Since leaving Hedo she had been wide awake with wonder at this exciting landscape, so different from the traffic-clogged environment where she lived.

"A small one," Carl qualified. "Like a cascade. You'll see. We'll go there. We're getting close now. There's a turnoff to the left. Hope we don't miss it."

The road rose into the hills, leaving the sea. Carl scoured the left side for the turnoff. "It must be farther than I thought," he said. They entered a crook in the road, made a little dip, and started rising.

"There!" They topped a rise and on their left was a narrow gravel road leading upward into the bush.

Flora stopped the car and eyed the lane doubtfully. "That looks rough, Carl. Do you think we can make it?"

"Sure. Want me to drive?"

The gully-filled gravel road was overgrown with weeds. Flora turned tentatively onto it, shifting into low gear as the car crawled over the rough surface criss-crossed with late-afternoon shadows.

As the road wound among trees and between walls of deep grass, Carl felt as if his being were trying to merge with his past, as though his past were one wheel and his present another, and the two wheels were overlapping. It should be hot and raining with him in the back of a big army truck with a dozen other church campers.

Flora's car rounded a sharp bend, returning Carl to the present. The road ended in a field of deep grass. A derelict concrete building stood to the left, beyond it a large pavilion crowded with weeds.

"Man, they haven't kept it up," Rick said.

"This is it." Carl happily sprang out of the car. The prospect might look bleak to the others, all weed-grown and abandoned, but to him it sparkled like quartz, a jewel into which he could peer and see—what? Besides, it had looked bleak to him the first time, too, in the mud and rain.

The others stiffly climbed out. "Mommy, I want to go home," Sharon said.

Carl laughed. "You'll see. You'll see. We're on a big cliff, like Hedo. Not as high. You see those trees over there? They're at the edge of the cliff. There used to be a trail going down to the beach. We'll make a new one if we have to. Down below there's the best beach you ever saw, completely secluded."

"Where do we pitch the tents?" Rick asked.

"I don't know. Let's look around first."

The rotting, wooden pavilion had holes in the roof, but the cement slab under it remained solid. Several old wooden picnic tables, half-rotten, sat among spider webs and dirt and stray insect bodies.

"I guess we ought to pitch the tents here by this pavilion," Carl said. His friends stood under the shelter, eyeing everything doubtfully. They did not know how alive it had been once, how the campers gathered here for their meals, buzzing with conversation and pausing for prayer, how the big green canvas tents brought the empty field to life like a circus in a parking lot.

Carl turned to Rick. "You didn't bring a machete, did you?" he asked.

Rick shook his head.

"Well, if we stomp the grass down, we can pitch the tents so they open right onto the slab, and then we won't have to walk in the weeds."

Rick started toward the car to unload it.

"I wish we had a lawn mower," Flora said with an uncertain giggle. Sharon huddled close to her, clutching her hand.

"Don't worry," Carl told her. "You'll love it, once you see."

● ● ●

Of course, they could not see how the big church truck chugged down the gravel lane and turned left onto the main road, which was steeped in late-evening shadows. A half mile down, between flanks of bush, the road bottomed out to a flat stretch with open beach on the left and the village of Sosu on the right. The villagers scurried about. The church campers had been invited to come and participate in some sort of celebration.

Carl stared out of the truck with interest, for up until now he had only seen the village in its ordinary, sleepy, day-to-day aspect—a few children, old women carrying clothes or vegetables, men working on their fishing skiffs, the young storekeeper sitting glibly behind the open counter of the little store.

Now there was a crowd of people, sturdy Okinawan men with stout arms and legs, women standing aside with clasped hands, children running around like hens. A big village drum had been brought out, and an old woman stood next to it. The men seemed to be struggling with some sort of giant sea serpent.

The truck rumbled to a stop in the open area in front of the store, and the crowd of campers climbed out. They were mostly American college kids from a church school in the States here to learn about missionary work, getting a taste of the exotic and hopefully learning that it was not all that it was cracked up to be.

The sea serpent turned out to be a massive hempen rope nearly a foot in diameter. There was going to be a tug-of-war involving all the men in the village, and the campers had been invited to join in. Men and boys clustered around the huge rope while girls and women stood back and the old crone beat the deep-toned drum.

Okinawan and American males intermingled equally on both sides. Women from the church camp stood around, chatting, not permitted to join. With a word the men lifted the astonishingly heavy rope. The entwined hemp was gritty with sand and slippery with mud. Carl sought for a good grip, lodging his feet in a strong stance.

Someone gave the shout to begin, and muscles strained. Loud moans, groans, and grunts came from both sides as the men struggled, grinning and frowning and gritting their teeth, first this side giving way, then that. Feet tended to slide in the dirt, and knees buckled as each man struggled to find new footholds, stronger grips. The gritty rope bit into hands, sand grinding under fingernails, palms rubbing raw. But it didn't matter. The object was to win.

At the peak of the contest a concerted silence descended on the scene, punctuated only by the thump of the ancient, upright log drum. One side began to give, moving forward a little, a little more, and then its strength was broken and Carl's side tugged the other team across the center line: victory!

A thunder of applause, laughter, shouting, and talk erupted. People shook hands all around, slapping each other's backs. Carl, with his buddies J.T. and Gerald, headed over to the store for something to drink. Carl bought a bottle of pineapple juice and went to sit in the cab of the truck with the door open. Watching the villagers, he realized he had been privy to a rare event.

Gerald sauntered over and leaned against the truck. "Do you know what that was all about?" he asked Carl.

"What?"

"It was a fertility rite." Gerald snickered.

"What's that?"

Gerald hesitated. "I'm not sure. I'm going to try to find out." He wandered off again. Maybe he had hoped Carl would know.

Later Gerald and J.T. came back over. Carl had been sitting in a peaceful lull, watching the happy commingling of clean-cut American college students with rough-hewn but polite Okinawan villagers in this remote corner of the earth. The dull sheen of the flat sea was flanked by a high-rising bluff on the left, and the narrow fishing skiffs appeared as black silhouettes in the dusk-silver sand.

"We found out what it means," J.T. said with a leer.

"What?"

J.T. and Gerald exchanged the conspiratorial glances

of adolescents discussing sex. "It means the winning side gets the women tonight," Gerald said. "They'll get to roll in the hay." Though a preacher's son, Gerald was notoriously profane.

"Wow," Carl said, his ethnological interest heightened. "You don't think we're supposed to . . . ?"

The boys stared at each other, mesmerized by the thought.

But as night fell, the church folks went back to their clifftop camp for hymn singing and prayer under the pavilion's electric lights.

CHAPTER 17

● ● ●

As the sun set among patchy clouds, Rick practiced karate in the open field. In front of their tents, pitched by the pavilion, Flora, Carl, and Sharon teamed up to cook supper on the camp stove.

The aroma of cooking food and the sound of cheerful voices formed an underlying texture in Rick's clean, empty mind. He grunted, kicked, punched, and blocked, his well-worn white uniform dampening with sweat, his frayed black belt flapping loosely at his waist.

He thought of an old Zen story that he had transmuted to a tale of karate. A master asked five of his students why they practiced karate.

The first student replied, "I practice karate so I can defend myself."

"Wonderful," said the master. "You will become impervious to attack."

The second student said, "I practice karate as a venerable tradition."

"Ah," said the master, "you will come truly to understand the meaning of the martial arts."

The third student said, "I practice to compete and win tournaments."

"Your honors will be many, your acclaim great," said the master.

The fourth student said, "I practice as a form of moving meditation."

"Excellent," said the master. "Your mind will become calm, your body fluid."

The fifth student said, "I practice karate to practice karate."

The master bowed, "I am your student!"

Rick smiled at the memory. No master had offered to become his student, but he believed he had finally reached the state of the fifth student. He had been through all the phases. Finally he discovered he had no "reason" to practice karate. He knew the principles of self-defense so thoroughly that they were wired into his nerves and muscles. He had studied the forms—series of karate movements handed down over the generations—and probed the traditions of ancient masters. He had won enough tournaments to fill his thick scrapbook with clippings. He had learned to open his mind while he went through his moves as though they were part of a sacred code.

And now with all that in the past? Or rather, now that it was absorbed fully into his being and no longer required his full attention?

Now he understood the meaning of karate, if indeed there could be said to be any "meaning." Now he practiced it to practice it and no longer troubled himself about purposes or goals.

The sun rested on the craggy hills, bathing the right side of his body as he shadow-boxed an imaginary opponent. Envisioning his opponent clearly before him, Rick performed his dance of fictitious violence. He parried punches, slipped deceptive foot attacks, and retaliated with hard stabbing kicks and brutal blows.

Keeping his body relaxed, his breathing rhythmic, he never stopped moving. His feet swept to his opponent's face, and his hands careened into the guy's chest, then hooked around to the head. The murmur of insects sounded like ancient crowds watching, staring, studying—crowds of spectators, of crickets, of grass blades—it didn't matter. The whole busy world. The clean, empty mind.

His body defied gravity's pull. Though a solid two hundred pounds, he had learned to renounce physical heaviness when necessary by floating his center of gravity into his chest, above its usual position below the navel. Thus he could spring, cover a great distance with effortless glides, and circulate like wind around his opponents.

Equally, he could weight himself down and become immovable. To do this he sank his center of gravity into his hips, channeling the force down through his legs and feet and into the ground like roots. His shoulders sagged from the boulder density of his body.

This worked well against foolhardy opponents who liked to charge him or tried to overwhelm him with a crazy barrage of techniques. If he sank himself solid, no matter how they threw themselves against him it was as useless as invaders attacking the Great Wall of China. He repelled them with the pure force of his stability. Then as they bounced off, he slammed his heavy kicks into their bodies with crushing strength.

Sometimes his imaginary opponents were not tournament competitors but serious attackers, muggers, robbers, killers. For them he used an entirely different arsenal of techniques.

He shattered their knees with low kicks and punched their eyes out with fingers stiff as blunt blades. He pummeled their windpipes, punctured their temples, and snapped their necks. His elbows burst their heads like melons, his knee torpedoed their chests, his shin paralyzed their thighs. With movements quick and economical, he needed none of the elaborate high-kicking flourishes necessary for tournament wins.

Personal safety no longer worried him once he

discovered that no one could hold him. He first became aware of this seemingly mystical ability during a self-defense drill in class. As he demonstrated how to get out of various holds, he found that by merely flexing his body he could send his attacker to the floor in an ignominious heap.

The techniques he had once relied on against grabs—stomps, rakes, elbows, palm strikes—became unnecessary. After class he had his strongest black-belt students practice grabs on him. He was right: a flexing motion of his chest and shoulders with an imperceptible torque of his hips sent the students flying. One astonished student said that grabbing him was like grabbing an electric eel.

Rick pondered the new phenomenon. He had trained long and hard to build his physique so that he could withstand virtually any blow and, if necessary, out-muscle his opponents. Yet now he didn't have to. When he asked his master about it, the old man just smiled and refused to comment.

Rick came to realize that these seemingly supernatural abilities were in fact as natural as sea wave or river flow. At last, somehow—through the endless practice of karate, of course—he had learned to harness his energy, his force, the totality of his muscles and nerves and lymph and skin and everything that made him a man, a human, a living being.

When his students laid hands on him, everything worked in unison. Naturally, they could not hold him, for they knew only how to use individual parts of their bodies—arms and legs, hands and feet and fingers. His sum was greater than their parts.

Now he understood how the master—much more accomplished than he—rolled so easily despite his age, tumbled like effervescent water, remained fluid and piercing and *masterful*. Compared to him, Rick still felt like a bumbling oaf, but he saw now that his body, mind, and soul had begun to absorb the lessons of karate.

He practiced karate to practice karate.

With the sun behind the hill, Rick seemed to come to consciousness from a deep slumber. He was still fighting, kicking and punching and blocking, but the imaginary opponent had gone. Rick's movements became superfluous.

"Rick!" Flora called. "Supper's ready."

Slowing his movements, Rick came to a halt and went through stretching exercises to cool down. Then he joined his friends.

● ● ●

That night as the tents stood like small cozy homes and a fire crackled, an unruly beauty possessed the place. The unseasoned campers had forgotten chairs, so Flora and Sharon sat side by side on the cement floor with their sleeping bags for a cushion. Rick leaned against a post near them, and Carl wiped the dew and condensation from the ice chest and made that his seat.

A wealth of deadwood edged the field, and Rick and Carl had dragged over enough to make a sizeable pile. Stars crammed the night sky, and a light mist rose from the deep grass, mixing with woodsmoke.

"Tomorrow we'll go down to the beach," Carl said. "It's beautiful. I remember one time they had a baptism down there. There's a pool in the shallows about chest deep, and the preacher baptized an Okinawan woman." He grinned. "The snorkeling is great. I wish we could go down there tonight and look at the stars and listen to the sea. The loneliest place on earth. Once we locate the trail, we'll go down there at night, tomorrow night maybe. You'll love it. It's one of the most beautiful places I've ever been."

"I'm not much of a camper," Flora admitted, "but this is nice."

As they stared at the fire, Carl became conscious of the utter silence around them.

He studied Sharon. The girl seemed unable to tear her eyes away from the campfire. Perhaps it was the first she had seen. "We're going to have fun, Sharon," he said.

Sharon did not reply. Her dark eyes reflected the flame in duplicate miniature. Her face was a rounder, smoother version of her mother's. She would be a beauty, like Flora, he decided.

"We'll swim—wade—in the sea, and in the pool with the waterfall," Carl went on. "You'll love it. And we'll go down to the village. They have a store there with cookies and pineapple juice. Sweetest pineapple juice I ever tasted."

He looked at Rick and Flora. Caught up in his own excitement, he could not guess how they might feel. But they seemed content and relaxed. "How do you like it, Rick?" he said, like a master of ceremonies.

"Nice." Rick shifted his weight against the post. "Real nice."

"You thinking about your classes?"

"Huh?" Rick, a tiger at rest, looked up at him. "No. Just remembering." He shifted again, each shift an adjustment deeper into relaxation. His eyes looked drowsy, drugged.

They must be sleepy, Carl thought. He wondered if he would be able to sleep. The wheels kept touching, the wheels of his past and present.

Flora yawned as Sharon leaned her head against her mother's side. "I think Sharon and I will turn in," Flora said. "Come on, honey." Grabbing the flashlight beside her, Flora stood and helped Sharon up. "Good night, all." They disappeared into the darkness with their sleeping bags. Carl heard the zip of their tent door and the rustle of them settling in for the night.

"Maybe I'd better turn in, too," Rick said.

"All right," Carl answered. "I'm going to sit up a while." He couldn't sleep now. He felt like a live coal, flared by the breezes of memory.

Rick stood. "See you later, buddy."

"Uh huh."

"You going to be all right?"

"Oh yeah."

Rick headed for the tent.

Happy to be alone now, Carl went over and sat in Rick's spot, leaning against the post. As if the place had some magical power, he too began to feel drowsy. A wonderful, all-encompassing peace spread through his body, out through his limbs, his fingers and toes, and up into his scalp.

He gazed into the fire, that warm, living thing that he loved. The smoke conjured up everything together, exposing the lie of time—the myth of past, present, and future. Carl felt it all merge together in the upward sigh of smoke, all the wheels turning, not separately, not overlapping, but in unison, one wheel. He was alone but not lonely, for at his back breathed a host of ancient ghosts, suffusing him with their presence.

A typhoon had been heading toward the island on that afternoon long ago. Carl had watched the gray curtain of rain being pulled back and forth across the sea. It never reached shore but stayed out in those glimmering, golden reaches, alloyed with the silver and pewter of the coming storm.

That night he had a huge six-man tent to himself—not everyone had arrived at the camp yet—and he lay in his cot unable to sleep because of the wind. A really strong, growling wind, it snapped the edges of the canvas tent over him, *whap whap*, keeping him awake. He'd lean over and tie one of the corners down, then another would blow loose. *Whap whap*. Wind blew through the tent, rustling his woolen army blanket, mussing his hair on the pillow.

At last he gave up. Gathering his bedclothes under his arm, he went out into the spitting rainy darkness and made his way over to the dark cone of a smaller tent. A three-man tent, it held only J.T. and Gerald, who were sound asleep.

In the darkness Carl nestled down on the empty cot in the snug, tied-down security of this tent. Outside, the wind howled and gnashed its rainy teeth. Carl fell into a cozy sleep.

Sometime in the night he heard voices, commotion. Half waking, he heard Hitachi-san, an Okinawan church member, trying to make himself heard over the force of the wind. Carl picked up the fact that Hitachi-san and family had arrived late, moving into the six-man tent Carl had vacated, and the tent had just blown down on them. Aroused from their sleep as well, Gerald and J.T. left with Hitachi-san to help the family find shelter. Carl turned over on his side, facing the musty canvas wall, and fell back asleep.

The next day was murky and gray, but the storm had passed on. The air felt cool and clammy. During the mid-morning lull after Bible study, Carl and J.T. sat on a table under the pavilion and J.T. played guitar. All those old, mellow folk songs. J.T. had a natural singing voice and knew how to finger-pick. The big guitar with its translucent, muted nylon strings made a lullaby sound.

In the late afternoon the clouds moved off, revealing patches of blue and gold. That night after supper Carl and J.T.—Gerald was spending his time with Sue Ann in those days—made their way down the trail with a flashlight and sat by the sea on the narrow strip of sandy beach.

When the tide came in, the water lapped right up to the base of the stone cliff, submerging the sand. When it went out, it left a great beach. Since it was coming in now, every so often they had to move back. Although the sky cleared, the sea still churned from the storm's agitation, and white-foamed waves encroached with sucking, hissing noises, its usual rhythm a bit off.

Carl lay on his back in the sand, looking at the stars. "Doesn't it make you feel like the end of the world is coming?" he asked J.T. "Like it could happen any minute? Like the heavens will roll back and there it will all be, Jesus and God and the angels with trumpets?"

The unending stars stretched infinitely at every angle, straight up and crossways and diagonally. The sky seemed like a big door behind which was heaven, God's palace. Underneath lay the vastness of the sea, its ruffled, starlit rug stretched over the length and breadth of the earth.

This beach was the ultimate sanctuary, yet it seemed precariously fragile, as though it would be the first place on which Jesus would set foot at his second coming. The end seemed so imminent: That sky would tear; the sea would suck down, crouching like an obedient whelp; the earth would flatten under the blazing glory. This little beach seemed the jumping-off place; beyond it stretched pure infinity. There was no sound except the sea, no sight except the stars. It was the end of the earth. The two boys lay there till they got sleepy, then headed back up the trail.

The next evening everybody trooped down to the beach for an open-air worship service. In the late dusk each chose a spot among the sand and rocks, little nooks and crannies, hard lava pews, and night fell while the preacher delivered a brief lesson. Then they sang hymns in the darkness. One person would strike into a hymn and everyone would follow.

For Carl, who felt the tug of adolescent cynicism, the service was nonetheless inspiring. True, he viewed his fellow humans with contempt, sneered at their petty attempts to commune with God, their vainglorious beliefs that they had the Almighty pegged. But out here where you couldn't see anybody and everyone was just a voice among the rocks, it was almost as though the stones themselves were singing, as though little gnomes who lived in the lava crevices had come out to chant praises.

On and on they sang—"How Great Thou Art," "Amazing Grace," "Trust and Obey," "Just as I Am"— the ones for which everybody knew the first verse. It was touching, these voices coming out of the darkness in unison.

Their presence eclipsed Carl's feeling of the impending end of the world. It was as if their gathering were staving off infinity, as if their songs not only praised God but held him at bay. Nestled invisible and anonymous in a cubbyhole of rock, Carl wished the others were all gone, that they had not come down here to his sanctuary, that he could sit in this spot alone and have the glory of God revealed to him. But it didn't happen.

CHAPTER 18

• • •

Next morning while Flora fixed breakfast with Rick acting as ranch hand and Sharon her apprentice chef, Carl did some exploring. He found the old outdoor latrine surrounded by waist-deep grass, snaky looking. Beating a path to it with a stick, he knocked down the cobwebs inside and brushed the dust off the weathered board seat with his handkerchief.

Across the field a trail had once led down to the beach, but now there were only weeds. He cast about like a hound, relying on memory and instinct to pick it up. About fifty feet out in the deep bushes at the far end of the field he came across what might have been a trail. Beating down brush as he walked, he entered a down-sloping stretch of woods and knew this was it. In the woods the trail was plain. Rainwater had kept it clear over the years, transforming the trail into a miniature streambed. He followed it downhill through belts of jungle and grass. The trees were short and gnarled, stunted by the shallow soil.

Coming out among sharp black rocks to the sea, his shoes touched the damp sand—the tide must be on its way out—and he walked around to the left. The wheels of past and present merged for a moment, and before the past wheeled away he strove to see J.T. sitting on the sand. Instead there were only a few empty plastic soft drink bottles. Trash—up here!

In contrast to his memory, the beach looked dingy and small. The sand seemed murky, the beach cramped, the cliff not nearly as dramatic as it should be. And what was trash doing here? It must have washed up from the south part of the island, or maybe the villagers at Sosu had taken to soiling their own nest like the rest of humanity. The sea, at least, looked right—clear and gorgeous.

Carl walked out to the water's edge, sniffing the salty tang, eyeing the mottled coral formations beneath the transparent water. Suddenly he felt lonely, abandoned. After all, he had no one, nothing—not even any place—to call his own. He stared at the sea and, with squinted eyes, tried to create someone. Sally maybe. Or the girl in Manila. Or Rosette, grown-up and beautiful.

Or Flora?

He had been evading the question for some time now. Could Flora be the one to fill the gap in his life?

Strange that Flora's rapport with Rick had aroused no jealousy in Carl. To the contrary, it almost soothed him, somehow.

Trying to envision the future—assuming he survived his current problems—Carl simply could not imagine Flora and himself on romantic terms. It was a nice idea; she was a pretty lady. Theoretically, a spark could be nurtured into flame. But he had to acknowledge that although he loved Flora as much as he had ever loved anyone, she did not ignite the sort of electric spark that Sally had. Love, not passion, ruled his feelings for Flora, no matter how lonely he might be at times. And he knew that she felt the same way about him.

So let it go, he told himself. Accept the fact that no one could fill his emptiness.

He ached like the sea must ache when the moon tugs

at it, longing to be transformed into lunar mist but able only to wallow in its vast, sandy bed.

He walked down the beach and found the pool where the Okinawan woman had been baptized many years before. On a whim, he stripped and waded into the water, maneuvering over the uneven coral and around spiky sea urchins. Reaching the edge of the pool, about five feet deep and as many across, he slid into its center. The water, captured in this cup of sand and coral, was heated by the sun.

Carl felt that he never wanted to leave this place, these northern hills and beaches. He was a writer. Why couldn't he write the life of Sosu—stay here, meet the people of the village, learn their ways, fish, garden, live under thatch?

Tiny fish pecked at his legs. Laughing, he waved them away.

Maybe if he stayed up here his old dream of the end of the world would finally come true. He simply had not waited long enough. He would have to station himself here and await the Second Coming. Ducking under, eyes closed, he splashed upward, snorting warm brine and laughing. There was no medicine like sun and sea.

Wading out of the water, he pulled on his clothes. Then he headed along the beach, back up the trail. He thought he heard a shout high on the breeze. He jogged up the trail, meeting Rick in the field.

"Did you hear me call?" Rick asked. "Flora's cooked a fantastic breakfast—coffee and bacon and eggs, plus cinnamon rolls."

"Great."

● ● ●

After they ate, they drove back up the road to the stream. A path led through deeply shaded, stunted forest. Its fragrances stirred the deepest wells of Carl's memory. As they neared the pool, they heard the rush of water and came out onto a broad rock ledge.

"How lovely!" Flora exclaimed.

The pool was enclosed by forest, fed by a gushing cascade that dropped through a chute of rock. "The shallow part is over there," Carl said. "You can go around the edge or we can carry Sharon across on our shoulders through the water."

"No," Sharon squeaked.

Carl smiled. "All right. We'll go around the side."

"There are no snakes in here, are there?" Flora said.

"Nah."

"It's deep here, isn't it?" Rick said, standing on tiptoe at the edge.

"Yeah. And over there is the diving rock." It was not as high as Carl remembered it, more like five feet than eight. "Come on, Sharon," he said, offering his hand.

She eyed him tentatively, looked at her mother for approval, then took the offered hand. Carl led her, with Flora behind, along the edge of the pool to a broad, open, shallow spot where a thin film of water slid over a bed of pebbles, dropping steeply to thread its way eventually to the sea.

Sharon released his hand and ran forward, up to her ankles in water. "It's cold!" she said, grinning. As her mother approached, Sharon pelted her with handfuls of water.

"Stop that, Sharon!" Flora said playfully.

Sharon squealed with delight. Then there was a massive splash as Rick dived in. They all looked up and he soon surfaced with his head slick as a seal's.

"Man, it's cold!" His voice echoed in the bowl of forest and rock.

Flora, goosebumpy and wet from Sharon's splashing, spread her towel on the flat rock and sat with her knees up. "It's nice in here," she said to Carl. The smells of mountain foliage filled the air like perfume.

Carl waded out, then swam across to the bottom of the cascade. Rick held onto a rock, peering up the white-water chute.

"Look at that," he said to Carl, his voice muffled by the crash of water.

"Fast, isn't it?"

"Wish it was smooth so we could slide down it."

"Have you tried the high dive yet?"

"No. Let's do it."

"All right."

Like schoolboys they swam to the ledge, clambered up the muddy slope and onto a small prow of rock.

"Here goes." Without hesitation Rick put his hands together and dove, an awkward, bearish dive.

"How is it?" Carl called when his friend surfaced.

"Great! Come on."

Tingling with anticipation, Carl counted to three and dove. The water greeted him in a harsh-soft embrace. Champagne bubbles surrounded him in the dark depths. He reached for the bottom but did not find it, turned, and thrust himself upward, emerging exhilarated. Rick had already scrambled up the bank.

Carl was climbing back up when Rick dove again, more skillfully this time, a sleek parting of the waters. He was under longer, and when he came up he said, "I did it." He blew water out his nostrils and shook his head to one side, clearing an ear. "I touched bottom."

"How deep?"

"I don't know. Must be eighteen feet, maybe twenty."

Carl dove. This time he made an effort for the bottom and found it, his fingers touching slick gravel, his eardrums aching with the pressure. Coming up, he thrust his head into the warm air. "Found it."

Flora stood, slender and pink in her one-piece navy suit. "You boys are having so much fun I'm going to have to try it." Tentatively, she waded out.

"Mommy!" Sharon cried.

"I'll come sit by you," Carl volunteered, crossing the pool with powerful strokes. Flora, up to her knees, looked skittish. "Oh, come on, Flora," Carl said. "Don't be such a sissy."

"I'm afraid of water."

"Go on in or Sharon and I will throw you in. Right, Sharon?"

Sharon looked alarmed at the mutinous thought. But Flora glided out into the water gingerly and began swimming with short, paddling strokes and upward kicks of her white soles. Carl pulled himself up beside Sharon and together they examined pebbles. The girl talked nonstop in a soft voice as she picked up pebble after pebble, studying each one, then either discarding it or adding it to a neat pile beside her.

"Want to dive?" Rick called to Flora from his rocky prow.

"I don't know," Flora said.

"Why don't you try it from that ledge over there first? Get used to it."

She paddled to the cascade and stared up the foaming chute. Rick dove in and swam to her. Carl could not hear their voices, muffled in the dense roar of water, but saw their two heads, one brown, one glossy black, as they floated side by side.

Then Rick turned and swam toward the low ledge, and Flora followed. As he clambered out and then helped Flora out, her pink-white skin looked stark against his big, brown, muscular body. She stood on the ledge beside him, diminished by his massiveness. Carl could just hear their voices.

"It's deep," Rick was telling her. "Just put your hands together and lean over. Push off with your toes. It's nothing from here."

"Here goes," she said, her voice quaking. Flora leaned out, but as she dove, she scissored her legs, trying to turn the dive into a jump, and flopped into the water on her side. She came up giggling. "That was dumb, really dumb!" she said in her schoolgirl voice.

Carl turned his attention to Sharon, her mother's young embodiment. He felt himself loving Sharon as he had loved Flora. In the background he heard Flora and Rick talking, laughing, diving, splashing, squealing. Their sounds faded in his ears as he and Sharon carefully amassed a precious collection of stones.

CHAPTER 19

● ● ●

After lunch and a nap, they walked down the trail to the beach. Carl led the way, carrying a bag of beach gear. Flora followed, picking her steps carefully. Rick carried a happy Sharon on his shoulders, ducking frequently to avoid low branches.

When they arrived, Carl was surprised to find the aura of dinginess gone. The sand, sun-dried white now, glistened, enhancing the sea's pure colors. And with the tide receding, the beach seemed spacious.

"Oh, Carl, this is gorgeous!" Flora said, her nervousness about the weed-grown trail apparently eclipsed by the sunny beauty of the spot.

"Didn't I tell you?"

"I want down!" Sharon cried, and even before her feet touched the ground they were moving. Running toward the water, she halted halfway and shouted, "Mommy, where's my bucket and shovel?"

The adults laughed at her enthusiasm as Carl handed her the toys. Flora spread a huge beach towel on the sand and sat down, her flip-flops set neatly to the side, lotion bottle ready to pour.

Carl and Rick kicked off their tennis shoes and pulled off their shirts, then put on flippers and waded out into the water, carrying their masks and snorkels. They stopped in knee-deep water to wash the masks.

"Reef doesn't look far," Rick said.

"It's not. You headed out there?"

"I thought I would. What about you?"

"I think I'll follow the shore for a ways. I want to explore these shallows."

"See you later, then."

Putting their masks on, they inserted the snorkels in their mouths and swam out.

Halfway to the reef, Rick stopped to see if the outgoing tide had any power. It didn't. He floated motionless. Then he went on until he saw the shallow wall of reef, colonies of compressed white coral. The water over it was just deep enough for him to skim over. Having his belly so close to the coral gave him a ticklish sensation. Then the sea floor angled down and sheered off to perhaps twenty feet. The drop produced a yawning sensation in his stomach. He would not have to swim far to be in deep water.

Rick rarely used his full strength snorkeling. Okinawan waters did not seem conducive to it. If he swam hard and fast, he would be out at deep sea in no time and would miss all the underwater sights. Snorkeling was more aesthetic than athletic. He glided slowly, giving a kick now and then, the big flippers boosting him forward with uncanny power. He floated for timeless periods, fascinated by the coral formations and sea life.

On impulse Rick turned upright, treading, and lifted his mask. The sea spread around him, opaque from this angle. The black cliff was tousled with jungle. He adjusted his mask and again submerged.

Rick did not fear sharks, not really. Shark attacks were virtually unheard of in Okinawan waters. But he knew that a fast-moving shark could appear in his circle of vision out of nowhere, abrupt and unstoppable.

Once before, swimming very close to shore at his

usual spot, he had detected a shadow off to his right and saw something dark and bigger than a man hurtle by just under the surface at incredible speed. It came and went so fast he could not identify it. Shark? Barracuda? Sting ray? Perhaps some species he knew nothing of. Perhaps some big, harmless fish.

In the clear water it was impossible to gauge depth accurately. He took a breath and dove. The water became cold and the pressure mounted swiftly in his ears. He worked his mask against his nostrils to equalize the pressure. Holding himself near the bottom by the force of his flippers, he looked up. It was like staring up a flight of stairs in a haunted house.

He propelled himself upward, at the surface blowing water out of his snorkel, tasting salt. How many body lengths was it? Six? Seven? Forty feet or so. Deceptive. From the surface it had looked deeper. He worked up his courage and swam farther out. Coral rose up like mushrooms, trees, brains, peacock tails. Solitary fish nosed about, and schools of tiny fish flickered past, fluid as mercury.

It had to be seventy feet deep now, maybe more. The water was noticeably cooler. As he swam, he wondered what it would be like to swim in water miles deep, peering into the blue-black abyss. What would lie beneath him?

When he felt certain he was floating above a depth of a hundred feet he stopped. This was far enough. The bottom was slightly blurry. He had never been so far he couldn't make out the bottom. It was something he wanted to do someday.

Why not today? What prevented him? What thin membrane in his mind did not want to be broken? There was no reason not to. He was not far from shore, not nearly as far as he had to go to reach the reef at his usual spot back home. Fifty, a hundred feet farther out and he would be there, over the bottomless blue.

He thought of Carl, sticking close to shore, crafty and safe, exploring the minutiae, the myriad visible wonders. That was understandable. Carl had not been here in ages. The waters were a renewed wonder to him. But Rick had been exploring safe limits for years. Wasn't it time to break out?

He thought of Flora and felt buoyant, as though she were a white float encircling him, making him safe, preventing any danger of sinking. She did not even like to get in the water, preferring to sun her white skin. Yet the thought of that land-bound woman gave him a hunger for the sea. He kicked his legs, moving out toward his limit.

It was silly to be nervous. Such depths were mundane to scuba divers. He knew some who went out past the reefs at night with lights. They had no fear. Crazy. It was not his element. His realm was the earth, the dojo. As a tiger depends on the jungle for camouflage and solitude, his abilities needed the gravity-solid earth to flourish.

The depth of the water beneath him made his adrenaline race. Rick allowed himself no fear. He did not want to send out fear vibrations, attract predators. Yet there was the thrill, excitement, daring, like when he was a young karate student learning to spar.

Conquering the fluttering in his belly and limbs and groin, he propelled himself again, just one kick of the flippers. A bit at a time, not too much. Already the ocean floor was growing fuzzy to his gaze, a dark blue cloud. He had been this far before, seen the floor look like this, but he had never ventured farther. This was where he had always turned back.

He hesitated now, needing something to boost him farther.

He floated like a jellyfish, victim of the current, afraid to lift his head from the water, afraid to see the ocean vast and mysterious, himself far from land. He needed to dismiss such thoughts, concentrate only on his circle of vision, his goal of going ahead.

Thinking of Flora again, he felt light and agile. He kicked forward. Just a few more yards. He had to squint to see the bottom. There were dark shapes down there that he did not want to think about. The water was cold; only a small circle of sun touched his back. A little farther, a few yards. He balked. How far out was he?

Flora. He pushed again. Again. Murky blue down there. Cold. Again. Flora. Shapes. Darkness.

Wouldn't it be something, now, here, to dive?

● ● ●

Sharon sat in the shallow water, playing, and squealed with glee.

"Well, what did you see?" Flora asked.

"Man! All kinds of stuff," Carl said. "I went way around the outcropping there. There're neat holes, and all kinds of coral."

"Where did Rick go?"

"He was headed out toward the reef. It's so nice out there. Don't you want to go?"

"No. I told you, I don't like swimming much."

"But Flora, it's so beautiful."

Flora cast a maternal look in her daughter's direction. "Sharon, you be careful! That coral will cut you."

"Do you like it out here, Flora? I mean really?" Carl asked.

"I love it. It's so remote."

"What do you think of Rick?"

"I like him. He's nice. Too bad I didn't know him back in high school. You should have introduced me."

"Funny, he was just a clumsy, bashful kid back then. He's so different now."

"He still seems bashful in a way. He's outgrown his clumsiness, I guess because of the karate."

"Yeah." Carl chuckled as they stared out over the blue sea, the hot afternoon sun only slightly mitigated by a breeze. "You and he sure seem to have hit it off."

"Oh, I don't know."

He looked over at her with a knowing smile. "Hey, I'm glad," he said softly.

She looked at him, and he knew from her eyes that everything between them was understood. "I do like him," she ventured.

"He's a good guy."

"Do you ever still—wonder?"

"You mean about you and me?"

She nodded.

He took a deep breath of the clean air and watched Sharon playing. "Not like that. I'm not sure I ever really did."

"Sure you did. We both did."

"Like you said, we were both under stress."

"It wasn't just that, though. Was it?"

"No."

"I'm glad it's all resolved now, though. Aren't you?"

"Definitely."

"One day you'll meet a woman who appreciates you for what you really are, like I do."

"Yeah, yeah, sure."

"You will, though."

He didn't answer.

"A therapist told me one time that I need unqualified love. I think that's what you always gave me. You needed love without the threat of a girlfriend. That's what I gave you. What do you think?"

He shrugged. "I don't know. Why have a reason, anyway, after all these years?"

Flora leaned forward. "Sharon, you're too far out! Come back in a little. That's a good girl."

"But Mommy, there's a fish."

"I don't care. That fish might bite you. Come back in."

"Don't tell her that," Carl admonished. "You're going to make her grow up with the same fears you have."

"Well?" She giggled. "It *might* bite."

He laughed. "True."

She put her hand up to shield her eyes from the glare. "I wonder where Rick is."

CHAPTER 20

● ● ●

Looking up from the dark closet of the sea floor, Rick saw the shape of a man floating on the silvery-blue surface. It would be Carl. Ready for air, Rick propelled himself upward from his deepest dive ever. He and Carl would chat, then swim together back to the reef.

But it wasn't Carl, Rick realized as he surfaced, gulping air. The man reached out as though to punch Rick lightly in the ribs, the sort of friendly gesture Carl might make. But this was no friendly gesture. In his right hand the man held a diver's knife, its point just inches from Rick's side.

In water Rick lost the advantage of quick reflexes. He thrust his arm down, twisting sideways, but it was too late. The tip of the blade drove into his side between the ribs.

Rick thrust downward with his elbow, ripping the blade from his side. As he reached for the knife, the man grabbed his hair with his left hand and pulled him back. Rick thrust both arms out, pinning the man's left arm between his forearms.

Perfectly positioned for the double-arm trap, Rick scissored his arms with every bit of his power, his whole being combined to snap the arm. It broke so easily at the elbow that the forearm wrenched backward nearly at a right angle to the upper arm. The man screamed and went limp.

Rick reached for the knife, but it twirled downward in a silvery wobble, sinking out of sight.

The man began to sink. Rick grabbed him by the hair and held the head up. The water around them was clouding with Rick's blood. He was dazed.

The whole affair had lasted less than a minute. His conscious mind still could not grasp what was happening. Some instinct told him to rescue the drowning man. It was as though he had forgotten the man tried to kill him, as though he had forgotten his wound. There was only a throbbing numbness in his left side.

Wrapping his arm under the heavy man's chin, he began to swim with difficulty. Unfamiliar with lifesaving techniques, Rick performed a sideways dog-paddle, struggling to keep the unconscious man's face above water, as well as his own. As he swam, he became aware of the quantities of seawater he had swallowed during the struggle. His belly felt swollen. Nausea choked his throat. Swimming exacerbated the flow of blood.

As he ran out of fuel, his head went under. He came up gasping, shaking the water out of his eyes, disoriented. He paused to catch his breath and locate the shore. He was not sure of anything anymore, of what he was doing, where he was going, whom he was rescuing.

The shore lay off to his left. He had turned parallel to it somehow. Changing direction, he hoisted the man on his hip like a sack of feed and stroked forward.

They seemed to advance in inches. The man lay across him like a dead horse. Rick's head kept going under. He wasn't sure why, whether he was losing consciousness or whether the man's weight pushed him under. The sky looked dark. Had night fallen? Had he blacked out?

He stopped to look for shore but couldn't find it, saw only globes of light, big purple spheres floating just above the water. They seemed like quiet, soothing rooms. Perhaps he could climb inside one and rest.

That's when he realized he could die—would die—if he did not do something soon. He had to decide and decide fast. He looked at the man and remembered the attack, the knife thrust, the wicked intent.

And he let go.

Suddenly he became buoyant and zipped forward in the water, propelled by his flippers. After a while he stopped and let his legs sink. His feet touched bottom. The water was only chest deep. He had passed the reef, though he couldn't remember having done so. He was safe.

But with that realization his strength deserted him. Shore still lay a long way off, and his blood continued to flow. Dizziness swamped him as he swam on.

He relied now on pure endurance—the tenacity that had allowed him to triumph in tournaments after a full day of fighting when his feet were bruised from opponents' heads, the same willpower that enabled him to suppress fatigue, fear, and pain and continue to fight.

The shore came closer, surrounded by brilliant globes of light. He stood and began to wade.

● ● ●

Rick collapsed in the sand just as Carl reached him.

Flora was right behind. "What's the matter?" She all but pushed Carl aside. "What happened?"

Rick curled in a ball and retched. His brown skin had an unhealthy yellow pallor. Because of his position they could not see the wound, but when he lay back Flora gently moved his arm, revealing a cruel, bloody gash in his left side, encrusted with sand.

"Sharon, take your bucket and fill it with water," Flora snapped. "Here, I'll do it." She grabbed the plastic pail from her dumbstruck daughter and hurried to the water's edge.

"What happened, Rick?" Carl asked. "Was it a shark?"

Rick shook his head. His lips were blue. "A man," he managed to say, rolling over again with the dry heaves.

Flora returned and dribbled the salty water over Rick's wound, washing away sand and blood. He flinched. "We need to get him to camp," she said.

Rick coughed and sputtered.

"Let him lie here a few minutes," Carl said. "He needs to get over being sick."

"I'm going up to get some drinking water and my first-aid kit."

"Would you rather I went?"

"No, you stay here with him and Sharon." But when she set out, Sharon followed tentatively. "Oh, all right. Come on, honey. Hurry!" Sharon bounded after her mother, who took her by the hand as they rushed up the trail.

Carl grabbed his beach towel nearby and dabbed Rick's cut. It was a nasty wound. "Can you talk now?"

Rick tried, but he was overcome with coughing. Carl knelt beside him patiently. The sun hung low and dark clouds were massing out over the sea. Carl scanned the water but could not comprehend what Rick meant by a man. Who? Where?

"It was him," Rick croaked. "Your hit man."

Carl's heart jumped. But he kept his voice calm. "Take it easy till Flora gets here," he said.

Rick shook his head. "I was way out, past the reef. Deep water. I dove, deeper than I've ever dove before. . . ." Another bout of coughing seized him. "When I turned to come up, I saw a swimmer . . . right above me . . . watching me through his mask. I thought it was you. When I got close . . he reached out. That's when . . . he cut me."

"How did he cut you?"

"He was holding a knife. I didn't see it at first. I wasn't expecting it. Stupid." He grimaced.

Flora returned with a large metal box, and Sharon followed with a water jug. Flora took the jug from her daughter. "Here." She held the jug to Rick's mouth. He took a sip and lay back.

"He said a man attacked him," Carl said.

"A man?" Flora stared at Carl, comprehension dawning in her eyes. He nodded. "Oh, Carl." She looked at Rick. "We've got to get him patched up and get out of here."

"Where is the guy now?" Carl asked Rick.

"Dead."

"That's enough for now," Flora said. "Let me tend to this wound. Rick, you just rest for a few minutes." She opened the box. Sharon stood nearby, watching wide-eyed.

A stiff, cool breeze gusted off the sea, chilly where they clustered in the long shadow of the cliff.

Flora poured disinfectant over the wound, patting it with a cotton ball, then laid an ointment-covered gauze strip over it. "Sit up if you can," she said. After drying his side with a clean towel, she taped the gauze into place. "I hope this holds. I'll fix a better one when we get back to camp. It's a nasty cut, but thank heavens it's not *too* deep. The main danger is infection. I hope the salt water helped cleanse it."

"Go ahead now, Rick. What happened?" Carl whispered.

Rick lay back, knees up, and stared at the sky. "He cut me and we grappled. At first it didn't click who he was or what was happening, only that he was trying to kill me. I managed to break his arm." He made a sound like a laugh. "Then, after I broke it right at the elbow"—he pointed—"I don't know, it's like he just passed out, I guess from the pain. He just slumped over in the water.

I could tell he wasn't faking because he dropped his knife."

"He must have been watching us from the beach, or from one of these cliffs," Carl said as though to himself. "When we split up, he thought you were me."

"I was bleeding kind of bad. I knew I had to get back fast. We were pretty far out. So I grabbed him around the neck and started towing him in."

"Towing him in?" Flora said. "You were going to save the man who tried to kill you?"

"I didn't do a very good job of it. I started getting sick. I swallowed a lot of seawater in the fight." He took a drink from the water bottle. "It was like waves of dizziness came over me, you know? Plus, I guess I was losing a lot of blood."

His voice was weak under the sighing wind. "Anyway, I could tell I was about to pass out. The guy—he was so heavy!" Anguish colored Rick's voice. He looked from Carl to Flora as if they were jurors. "If it had been anyone else. . . . But I knew he was the one who wanted to kill you, Carl. And he'd tried to kill me."

"So you let him go," Carl said.

Rick nodded.

"Good!" Flora said. "I never would have tried to save him in the first place."

"How far out were you when you let him go?"

"I don't know. Seemed like a long way. I still nearly didn't get back. I thought I would black out for sure. God was with me."

Carl stood and scanned the water but saw nothing. The sea was growing choppy under the wind. "You did the right thing, Rick," he said. "It was noble for you even to consider saving him. I wouldn't have. I don't know anyone who would. Anyway, I'm glad you're alive, pal. I'm just sorry it was you he attacked."

Flora laid her hand on Carl's shoulder. "Be glad. He's the karate expert." She looked at Rick's side. "Oh, no!"

The bandage was stained with blood. "We need to get you to the car, Rick. That wound needs attention."

"Come on," Carl said, slipping his arm behind Rick's back. Rick stumbled to his feet and Carl helped him up the trail as Sharon and Flora followed with the gear.

CHAPTER 21

• • •

"What should we do about the tents and everything?" Flora asked after they had helped Rick into the back seat of the car.

"Leave them," Carl said. "We can come back and get them later. Let's get out of here."

Ever since he had seen Rick stumble out of the water, he'd been possessed with a panicky foreboding. It will never end, he told himself. Despite all their precautions, all their cleverness, violence had sought them out, pursuing them to the nethermost regions of this island paradise. Just when they thought they had finally eluded its grasp, it struck with bloody, unexpected force.

Further, Carl recoiled to see Rick, whom he had come to regard as virtually invulnerable, so devastated. That man who walked with an easy, relaxed gait, utterly confident, with nothing to prove, had staggered ashore bloody, pale, and weak.

As Carl got behind the steering wheel, Flora and Sharon crammed into the passenger seat so Rick could stretch out in back. At least they were getting away now. The killer was floating face down at sea, and they would speed away in this car to sanctuary at last. Carl should have been elated, but driving down that gravel lane he felt only gloom and fear.

"We need to hurry," Flora said. "Rick needs medical attention."

He accelerated as they sped around the bumpy turns. When they approached the main road, he hit the brake pedal, but his foot went to the floor. "Hold on!" he shouted. The car soared across the road and crashed into a ditch, slamming to a halt against the bank.

Sharon began wailing like an ambulance siren.

"Is everyone okay?" Carl said. He had cut his lip on the steering wheel. He tasted blood.

Flora seemed to shake away her own pain as she brushed back her daughter's hair to examine the bump on her forehead. The child continued to cry, but softer now.

Carl turned. "Rick, are you all right?"

Rick pulled himself up from the back-seat floor. "I'm all right," he said, holding his side.

"What happened, Carl?" Flora said angrily. "Why didn't you stop?"

"No brakes." Pressing a handkerchief to his mouth, he got out and opened the hood. Then he got down on his hands and knees and peered under the car. After a few minutes he stood. "The brake line's nicked. Looks like someone may have cut it."

"Can you fix it?" Flora asked after an astonished pause. Sharon's crying had subsided.

Carl shook his head. "We need a mechanic." He looked around. The wind whipped around him in a fury, and gray clouds covered the sky. A storm was coming.

"Is the car banged up very bad?" Flora asked.

He walked around it to look. "The bumper's smashed, and the fender on your side is dented. Nothing serious. We can drive if we can just get the brakes fixed. I guess I'd better walk down the road to Sosu. Maybe they have a mechanic."

"We'll wait for you here." Flora stroked Sharon's hair.

Carl took a few steps, then returned. "I just remembered. I don't speak the language."

Flora turned around in the seat. "Rick, will you be all right here if I go with him?"

He nodded.

"Wait. Let me see your wound. Here. Apply pressure, like this," she instructed. "Don't let up for five minutes. Maybe they'll have a doctor in the village. If not I'm going to bandage that up thoroughly. Come on, Sharon."

She got out, toting the girl on her hip. "Let's go, Carl." As the three set off down the road, they were peppered with wind-blown grit, and thunder echoed from the halls of the sea.

● ● ●

Less than a half-mile from the car the road cut through the hills and opened out to a beach on the left with the village on the right crammed up against the side of a mountain. It looked exactly like it did in Carl's memory, except that the store had grown from a mere outdoor stall to an actual building. He had no time for memories now. This day belonged to a new world, one that did not allow him the luxury of reflection.

The choppy sea gleamed malevolently, and the wind off the ocean struck them full force as they crossed the gravel parking lot to the store. Inside, a young Okinawan man was preparing to close up shop.

Flora greeted him in Japanese.

"Tell him we need a mechanic," Carl said. "Tell him our brake line needs replacing, and we need brake fluid."

She translated.

With an apologetic grin the man shook his head as he answered, clucking his tongue.

"He said there is a mechanic, but he's gone to another

village and won't be back till morning," Flora told Carl. She asked another question and got a similar response. "No doctor, either." She thanked the man and they went out.

"What do you want to do?" he asked. It was getting dark fast.

"I don't know, Carl. I just don't know. What can we do?"

"I guess we should go ahead and camp for the night. At least the tents are set up," he replied. "In the morning we'll come back down here and find that mechanic, get him to fix the car, and head back south. Do you think Rick will be okay?"

"I'm going to bandage that wound right," she said determinedly. "I didn't have time at the beach. He'll be all right once I get it fixed properly."

"I didn't realize you were such a good nurse."

She smiled grimly. "Mothers have to be a little of everything."

"It's a good thing you had that first-aid kit."

"I never go anywhere without it." She nudged him playfully, and the gesture lifted his spirits.

The car, nose-down in the ditch by the roadside, looked derelict and sad, like someone else's tragedy. Rick had gotten out and leaned morosely against the car. "Well?"

"No luck," said Carl. "Mechanic won't be back till morning. No doctor. We decided we should just walk back to camp. Is that all right with you? Can you make it? It isn't too far."

He nodded. "I think I need to lie down for just a minute first, though."

After a short rest for Rick, Carl put his arm under his friend's shoulders, and they headed up the lane.

Back at the campsite, after numerous stops to rest, Flora set to work immediately. "Carl, why don't you build a fire while I work on Rick?" she said. "Sharon, you help me. We're going to be doctor and nurse, all right? You're the nurse." She began rummaging through the first-aid box, then looked up. "If you can, Carl, maybe you'd like to fix us something to eat on the stove. Rick needs some food. I brought some packages of instant hot chocolate, and there's a couple cans of vegetable-beef soup in there. That's just what he needs, isn't it, Sharon?"

"Yep," she agreed.

Rick stretched out on his sleeping bag in the tent, and Flora knelt beside him.

Carl heard her cheerful nurse talk as he built a fire and heated soup on the stove. As it simmered, he stepped out of sight and changed into dry clothes, then returned to the fire, which the wind was whipping wildly about. He stood beside the blaze, poking it with a long stick.

Flora emerged from the tent. "Soup ready? I smell it."

"Sure is."

"Good. Let me have a cupful for Rick, please."

Scooping up a cup, Carl gave it to her, and she disappeared into the tent. The fire threw a cozy glow on the campsite as darkness surrounded them. Carl sat on the ice chest, imagining the hit man, bloated and blue in the sea. He dodged the thought. He wasn't ready to contemplate that yet. Maybe when they were out of here, safe and sound. . . .

Things still weren't right, with Rick hurt and the car broken down. And the brake line—the killer had to have cut it. What a nasty trick. If he had wanted to prevent their leaving, he could have taken the coil wire or sliced the brake line clean in two. But it was nicked, so the brake fluid wouldn't drain out until he had hit the brake a few times and made a few turns—in short, until they were in motion on the road. Sadistic! The killer had planned the accident, knowing a woman and child were along.

He must have sabotaged the car while they were at the beach—slipped up, cut the line, then found a place where he could watch them on the beach, probably through binoculars. Having seen Carl and Rick swim out together, he must have confused the two from the distance. Then he sneaked down to the water, out of sight up the beach, and swam out, planning to kill Carl at sea.

It was smart, Carl had to admit. A dead body at sea would mean less chance of being caught. Even if the body washed ashore, days could have passed, giving the killer ample time to escape.

Chills snaked down Carl's spine as he contemplated the hit man's plot. What if he hadn't made that mistake? What if Carl had been swimming idly in the shallows and the man appeared, armed with a knife? Carl had left his own knife on shore.

But the killer had not reckoned on tangling with a karate expert. Despite being caught by surprise in deep water, Rick's karate skills had saved him, evening the odds.

Carl tried to imagine the fight, the mortal combat at sea. He doubted he could have survived such an ordeal. And yet Rick, with all his injuries, had made an effort to save the man. What could they have done with him had Rick succeeded? Turned him over to the police, no doubt. But that would have been less than desirable. Sooner or later he would get out—probably after thirty days or so in the can on an aggravated assault charge. And then he'd be hot on the trail again, more determined than ever.

No, it had worked out perfectly for Carl. He wondered whether they should report the incident to the police. Even if the man's body were discovered, it would be impossible to determine what had happened. Cause of death: drowning. His broken arm would be the only red herring, and after several days of bloating and soaking at sea, that might not even be noticeable. Sharks might finish off the body, too. There had been plenty of blood to lure them in.

Carl looked up as Flora crawled out of the tent with the empty cup. "I think he's falling asleep," she said quietly. "That's what he needs more than anything, rest. The soup will help, too. Thank you for fixing it." She kissed his cheek. "I'm sorry if I was grouchy to you before."

He smiled. "How about the hot chocolate?"

"Sharon and I might take some after we've had our soup. What do you say, Sharon?"

The girl was sitting on the pavilion floor playing morosely with some sticks. She looked at her mother with mournful eyes and nodded.

Flora rummaged through the food box. "Oh, look. Marshmallows," she said. "After we eat our soup, maybe we can toast some marshmallows. Would you like that, honey?"

Sharon nodded again.

"She's awfully sleepy," Flora told Carl. "Want some soup?"

"Sure."

Flora dished out a cup of soup for each of them while Carl opened a package of crackers. They ate without talking.

"It looks like we've got a storm coming," Flora said, setting her bowl down. "Do you think these tents will hold?"

"I think so."

"Look, Sharon's about to fall asleep. Do you want to go to bed, honey?" The girl shook her head drowsily. "Sure you do. Come on, let Mommy put you to bed. I'm going to let you skip brushing your teeth just this once, okay?" She put their dishes into a pan of water and led Sharon into their tent.

Carl boiled water for hot chocolate. When Flora came out, he handed her a steaming mug.

"Thanks. She's asleep already, poor thing. It's been a rough day for her, too."

"I'm sure."

"It's going to be okay now, Carl. It really is."

"I know." He sat on the ice chest, his hands cradling the comforting warmth of his mug.

Flora sat beside him on the ground, knees up, like an alpine skier in front of a roaring fireplace. "Rick is the one who's really suffered. And you. I haven't forgotten about you."

"What about you?"

"Me? I've had fun. I got to play nurse." She grinned at him, then returned her gaze to the fire.

"You did a good job of it, that's for sure."

"Thank you." She set the mug down. "Carl, I would love to stay up with you and talk, but I just can't. My eyes won't stay open. Is that okay?"

"Sure."

"Finish my chocolate if you like. There's half a cup left. I'm sorry. I'm just exhausted all of a sudden."

"Go to bed. I'll put everything away."

"Thank you." She stood and stretched. "Don't worry about anything, all right?"

"I won't."

"Good night."

"Night."

She climbed into her tent, and he could hear her speak soothingly to Sharon as she nestled into her sleeping bag.

Carl stared at the fire as he finished his drink. Then he lit his meerschaum pipe and puffed thoughtfully. He was tired too. The gloomy foreboding had left him. He felt almost peaceful. It is finished now, he thought. All over. I'll go to bed and wake up and get the car fixed and we'll all go home. Live happily ever after.

After cleaning up the dishes and putting everything away, he climbed in beside Rick. His friend's deep breathing soothed Carl. Pulling up his sleeping bag, he closed his eyes and listened to the sighing wind.

CHAPTER 22

● ● ●

Rick sat up in the night with a shout, the spirit-cry of karate fighters. "He's alive!" he said.

"What?" Confused, Carl raised his head. A steady rain drummed on the tent.

"He's alive."

Carl wondered if Rick was talking in his sleep. His voice did not sound normal. "Who's alive? What do you mean?" Carl sat up.

"He's alive. The man. He's not dead."

"How do you know?"

Rick lay back. "I had a dream." His words slurred together. "I dreamed he's alive—the killer."

"How could he be alive, Rick? He had to have drowned."

"I don't know. I just felt it."

"What was your dream?" Carl's chest constricted in a python grip.

"It's hard to describe. I can't . . ."

Although Carl had told himself it was over, somehow he had known it wasn't. "Rick," he whispered. "Rick."

"Mmm."

"Are you asleep?" Carl's heart bashed against the walls of his chest.

"Mmm."

Hands shaking, Carl threw off the sleeping bag, unzipped the tent, and crawled out, gasping for air. He sucked the wind, drank it.

Grabbing a flashlight, he stumbled away from camp, out into the meadow. Could the hit man still be out there? Rain pelleted him, cruel shots from a malicious world. Gagging, he struggled out of his shirt, fell to all fours, and became sick.

Fear roared through his body like a fire storm. He slid forward into the wet grass, his skin feverish. Rain stroked his back with tinselly fingers. His nausea abated, but fear crawled inside him like hermit crabs patrolling his innards. He rubbed his face in the clean grass, his hair plastered with water.

The cold rain slapped him out of his spell. He stood up and looked for his shirt but couldn't find it. Maybe the wind had stolen it. Thunder rumbled under the skin of the world.

He set out across the meadow. In the thin cone of his flashlight beam he saw the grass pushed flat, its matted underbelly exposed to the wind. Bits of leaves and twigs flew through the air. The rain stung his skin.

Finding the trail, he headed down through the woods. If the man was alive, as Rick had dreamed, Carl wanted to find him, face him, get it over with. He could not get it out of his head that the man was down there on the beach, waiting, planning his next assault. Carl was ready to do battle, his terror hammered into rage.

His bare feet slid out from under him, and he slammed down onto his back. For one irrational moment, he thought he'd been intentionally tripped. He braced for an attack. When it didn't come, he struggled to his feet and continued downhill, gripping his flashlight like a weapon.

Carl heard the slosh of waves as he approached the beach. In the flashlight beam the sea was a black, angry surface, opaque as stone. The wet sand clung to his feet. The tide was coming in and wasting no time about it.

He clicked his light off. The wrath of God surrounded him, pure, unfathomable anger the prophets had understood. The killer must be an instrument of divine malice, he realized, an arrow from God's bow targeted at Carl. He imagined the corpse in those sizzling waves, bounding on the tide, arm dangling askew, face contorted in a blue grin, body swollen to abnormal size, drowned but still alive, unkillable, coming this way, backed by sea and storm.

No! Carl clawed at his chest in fear. A freak wave doused him, cooling his hysteria. Then he saw a light. His mind congealed into cold, determined purpose as he saw the single flashlight beam far down the beach. The hit man was here after all, and at Carl's mercy. Carl patted his pocket. The butterfly knife nestled there securely, his ever-faithful mistress.

Carl took a deep breath. He would have to hurry before the encroaching sea blocked his progress and trapped him against the wall of cliffs. The approaching tide murmured threateningly. He jogged down the beach.

The sand ended and a spur of rock barred his way. He realized the light was not on the shore at all but out in the water. A swimmer? Boat? He was tempted to shine his light out there to look but did not dare give away his presence. It could be the killer, washed up on a spit or rock, recuperating, waiting.

He remembered now that there had been a rocky pinnacle out there in the water, well down the beach from where they had snorkeled. A mushroom-shaped crag of sharp, black rock, it was scarcely ten feet across. In low tide the stem of the mushroom was visible, but in high tide the water would approach the crown. Who could be out there now in this weather?

The beam of light bobbed erratically. It made no

sense. It had to be the killer. He had made it to the rock and climbed up there. But what was he doing with a flashlight? Maybe the rock had been his hideout as he watched. . . .

Enough thinking! Taking just a moment to brace himself, Carl waded out. The coral tore brutally at his feet but wasn't as fierce as the driving water. It surged to his knees, to his waist. A wave higher than the rest smashed him in the face. He came up sputtering, his flashlight gone, ripped from his hand. "All right!" he said angrily, plunging forward.

The world was water, a flood of rain and brine. As he swam into the turbulent waves, his only point of reference in the whole, chaotic world was that beam of light up ahead.

There was no up or down, just engulfing, howling, savage blackness. Crazy words sprang into his head, a passage from an old Sunday school lesson: "Fire and heat! Ice and snow! Light and darkness! Lightning and clouds! Mountains and hills! Seas and rivers! Sea beasts and everything that lives in water! All bless the Lord: Give glory and eternal praise to him, for he has snatched us from the underworld."

Carl wondered if God would snatch him from the underworld into which he had hurled himself. Sudden, intense fatigue made him wonder what he was doing. Was he going to do what the killer had failed to do? Snuff out his own life? This was insane!

Bobbing up and down in the waves, he looked around for the shore. There was no sign of it in the darkness, only that flashlight beam. If he just floated, the tide would carry him in, most likely, assuming he didn't drown.

But the light beckoned. He set out again, pitting all his sinewy muscle against the gathering wrath of the sea. The waves held far less than typhoon strength or he'd have never made it this far. But they were powerful enough to make him fear for his life.

With a shock he realized he was almost at the rock, for the light was a small one. He heard waves crashing against stone. He paused to reconnoiter, but the water threw him about mercilessly. The light played about on the surface, passing near him. He felt a fearful suction: whirlpool! He tried to swim back but, exhausted, got nowhere.

He had no choice but to cry out. "Hey!" he shouted. "Hey!"

The light stopped suddenly, swung carefully back, and stopped on his bouncing head.

He waved his arms in the rain. "Hey!"

His only hope was to make for the rock fast, swim in the direction of the current, and hope it wouldn't suck him under.

Something large brushed against him in the water. He reached out instinctively to push it away. To his horror he realized that it was a human body.

He screamed. Every cell in his body came alive with pure terror, every muscle contracted, every nerve writhed like a beheaded snake. He pushed away and was caught in the vortex of the mushroom rock. Its hungry current wrapped like a tentacle around his feet.

In blind, choking panic he swam toward the rock. A wave caught him and smashed him into it, bruising his shoulders and ripping his skin. It smashed him again, and he felt strong fingers grip his hair, then his chin, struggling to pull him up.

He was caught in a vise. The water had his body; those hands had his head. His neck would snap. But with the next wave he shoved upward with his feet and caught the rock with his hands. Aided by invisible arms, he dragged himself up over the sharp rock, lacerating his body, ripping his trousers, slashing his legs.

He rolled to his feet and fumbled for his knife. The

flashlight blinded him. His hand snagged in the wet pocket, tearing it. The knife dropped down inside his pants leg.

That's when he saw the young woman behind the flashlight. She seemed as shocked as he. Then a little boy, perhaps six years old, materialized in the dim light, grabbing his arm.

The woman was shouting in a language he could not understand.

Carl groped for his knife but couldn't find it. Only then did he realize he was standing inches from the edge of the rock. That was why the boy was tugging him. Carl lunged forward and the boy and woman both pulled him safely to the crown of the rock.

By the light he saw that both were Okinawans, villagers by their dress, though their clothes were drenched. The woman's eyes gleamed with terror.

"I saw your light," he said, shouting to make himself heard. "What are you doing here?"

"Our boat hit rocks," she replied, her English halting, unsure. "It broke. My husband . . ." She shook her head and bit her lip as the rain streamed down her face.

Her husband! That was the corpse floating at the base of the rock, held in place by the slow, sucking whirlpool.

"You have boat?" she asked.

He laughed. A boat! Pain made him look down, and he discovered his chest slashed in a number of places, his pants in shreds. The woman reached out with the hem of her soaking blouse and dabbed one of the cuts on his chest. Then she pointed out to the water and made motions of it splashing over her.

"Up here?"

She nodded. "We die." She pulled her boy to her.

His body tired and battered, Carl's mind kicked into gear. All his previous fears—they seemed so petty—vanished. They had to get out of here. He had swum out. He could swim back. But what about these two?

"Here, let me see." Carl took the light from her and played it across the water. The prospect was dismal: angry black water stretching into darkness. "Which way's the shore?" She pointed, but he could not make it out in the heavy rain.

He spotted an oblong shape in the water, thought first it was the dead husband, then recognized it as a board, part of the shattered boat. "Look!" he exclaimed.

"Not big," she said, her voice without hope.

She was right. He continued to scan the water, looking for any sort of floating detritus. Nothing. The rain pelted down afresh, scouring them with its vicious cold. The woman huddled down, hugging the boy. She cried out as a monstrous wave soaked them with brine.

"Can you swim?" Carl asked.

She shook her head, terrified.

"Can you swim?" he repeated.

"Yes!"

"Can he?"

She looked at the boy. "Yes."

Carl looked back at the board, tossing in the waves, farther away now. "Come on."

"No!"

"Come on!" he shouted furiously. He picked the boy up and slung him under his arm, grabbed the woman roughly by the wrist, and jumped.

They went under. Carl's two companions dragged him down like anchors. He thought they would never come up. Suddenly they surfaced, gasping.

"Kick!" Carl yelled.

The whirlpool sucked at their heels.

"Swim for it!" he hollered. Letting them go, he surged forward. Then his hand bumped the board. "Here! Grab this! Over here!" The woman appeared beside him, latching onto the board.

"Seiku!" she screamed.

Carl heard a cry near him. He reached out into the

blackness, hit something—grabbed. It was Seiku's arm. He pulled the boy roughly to him.

"Now, kick toward shore!"

Gripping their tiny raft with desperate fingers, they battled toward an unseen destination. Propelled by sheer panic, they burst free of the rock's suction, and the waves mounted at their backs to push them forward like surfers. They rode high and fast, and in no time they felt coral scrape their shins, and sand under their feet.

Holding one another's hands, they struggled to shore and crossed the beach, picking their way blindly among the rocks till they felt the ground slope upward and grass brush their ankles. Well away from the water, they dropped to their knees, huddled together, shivering and coughing.

Carl's body came afire with pain. His chest heaved from the exertion. Now that it was over he was a weak, sick man. He lay down.

"Wait," the woman said in his ear. "We go for help."

Then she and the boy were gone.

CHAPTER 23

● ● ●

In his dreams he walked an uneven landscape, buffeted by invisible shoulders and arms, tugged by hands of ghosts. It was a hellish terrain, mired in blackness, crowded with thorns and sharp stones, shrieking with wind and rain. He tripped and banged his knee. Hands pulled him to his feet and dragged him on.

Scorpions of pain crawled over his body, whipping him with their tails. He surrendered to the pain and ceased to walk. Something hoisted him, and he sensed movement. Then he dropped a long, long way into sleep.

In his dream he was in Flora's living room at Kadena Circle. Sharon sat on the floor, coloring while Rick and Flora were engaged in animated conversation—but Carl could hear nothing. He seemed deaf. They turned toward him, smiling, as if they had asked him a question and awaited an answer. He looked from one to the other in blank confusion. Rick laughed soundlessly and punched Carl playfully on the shoulder. Flora, grinning, squeezed his other shoulder affectionately.

Carl's eyes flooded with tears. He reached out like a man adrift and threw an arm around each of them, clasping their necks like life buoys. Showing no surprise, they moved close to him, Flora slipping her arms around him to embrace him while Rick encircled them both with his arms protectively. Sharon, joining in, held onto Carl's trouser leg.

Carl wept within their circle, a rainstorm of tears, and slowly the silence that encased him slid away to the gentle noises of someone moving about in a room.

He opened his eyes to the glow of a lantern. A wizened old man, his goatee a wisp on his deeply lined face, looked over with eyes slanted and gleaming. Carl tried to sit up. The man smiled and pushed him gently back down, rearranging the blanket around his shoulders.

Carl relaxed. With this man here, there could be no danger.

● ● ●

Morning light brought him to his senses. A rooster crow. Woodsmoke. Smells of tea and fish. He sat up.

Carl lay on a simple cane bed in a small hut. Pulling the blanket away, he found his chest covered with bandages. A broad strip of cloth had been wrapped around his waist like an ankle-length skirt. His trousers were gone.

The old man brought him a bowl of rice and fish and a cup of steaming tea. Carl sipped the tea and struggled with chopsticks, managing to eat.

After giving the dishes back, he murmured his thanks, but the old man just shook his head and turned away.

Walking outside, joints stiff and painful, Carl discovered a world he had never seen before. Two huts and a shed were set in a clearing in the hills, surrounded by immaculate gardens and, beyond them, forest. Pigs rooted in a pen. Chickens scratched in the dirt. Wind gusted across the blue sky.

"You are okay?" The young woman appeared beside him. She looked like she had been crying.

"I am sorry about your husband," Carl said. His words came slowly, as if his thoughts had been rearranged in the night.

She could not reply.

"And your son, how is he?"

"Okay. Only you hurt." She motioned to his bandages.

"Thank you, or whoever bandaged me."

She nodded.

"It looks like you saved me."

She managed a smile. "You saved *me*," she insisted.

"What is your name?"

"Sachi. You?" She pointed at his chest.

"Carl Connolly."

"You have eaten?"

"Yes."

"My father, Uza-san, help carry you to house."

"I hardly remember it."

"You were not . . . awake." She had to search for her words. "Why did you swim to rock?"

"I told you. I saw your light."

"I thought you had boat. Why you swim?"

He laughed as he remembered. Some crazy delusion from another life had told him that an assassin waited for him on that rock. Assassin! Yet he had found these people—real human beings, not phantoms. The discovery seemed to have restored a certain order to Carl's life, as if he had awakened from a nightmare or recovered from a grave illness. He smiled at the woman, who returned his smile and looked away.

Carl heard a shout and looked up to see the little boy race toward him. Carl grinned and tousled his hair. "What is your name?" He looked at his mother, who translated.

"Seiku," the boy said proudly, looking at him with bright eyes.

"Oh yes. Seiku. I am Carl." He held out his hand, and they shook solemnly.

They walked down a path among the gardens, through rich, rain-washed air.

"Where you come from?" Sachi asked.

Carl remembered Flora, Sharon, Rick. "A camp near Sosu. I need to get back there immediately. They won't know what's happened to me."

Sachi stopped in the middle of the path. "You have someone there?" she asked.

"Yes. Friends." A dreamlike quality possessed him. Carl felt like a stranger to himself. He wore odd clothing and was in an unknown place with unfamiliar people. He had awakened in a new land, a strangely peaceful one.

"Look," said Sachi. "Our river."

Carl looked up to see a small stream a short distance away, gushing down the hill among rocks and a profusion of plants such as elephant ear and bamboo. Carl squatted by the clear stream, splashing water onto his face.

Sachi knelt beside him. Scooping water with her palms, she drank. Then she looked at Carl.

He scooped handfuls into his mouth. The silvery water sent a cold, vibrant glow through his body. Unaccountably he began to cry. Sitting down on a nearby rock, he let the tears flow, oblivious to the woman and her child.

He seemed to sit there a long time. A gull flew overhead, riding the strong wind. Bamboo cast linear shadows across the stream. Tiny fish darted in the shallows. A handmade toy boat lay on its side in the gravel. Carl reached for it.

The boy saw him and came to his side. Saying something in Japanese, he pointed at the boat then back to himself, proudly.

"So you made this," Carl murmured. He set the boat

into the water and smiled at the boy. Seiku nodded, so Carl let go. The boat drifted downstream, swirled around a fast bend, and coasted out of sight among the weeds.

The boy chased after it.

"He not know his father dead," Sachi said sadly. "He thinks he come back."

"How did you get on the rock?"

"We see family on Yoron Shima. You know?" He shook his head. "A small island," she explained. "Storm came and boat . . . hit rock. My husband . . . he pulled us to rock. We get on, but wave comes, takes him . . ." She turned away, hands to her face.

"I'm sorry."

She gathered herself. "I am to thank you."

He smiled gently. "You live here?"

She nodded. "And my father," she said.

"Is he a fisherman?"

"No. Farmer. My husband . . . he fisherman."

"What will you do now?"

She sighed and squatted a few feet away. "Find my husband. Bury him in family tomb." She stared at the running stream. A strand of black hair fell across her forehead. She looked at Carl. "We must pay you."

"Pay me?" He laughed.

"It is custom."

"You've already paid me. You saved my life."

She shook her head vigorously.

"Sachi, you owe me nothing."

She stood up. "You are wrong."

Seiku came crashing upstream through the bushes. He shouted something in Japanese to his mother, and she replied. Then he asked something—about his father, Carl could tell, as pain flashed across the woman's face.

Sachi took her son's hand and turned to go back to the

house. Carl stayed where he was, transfixed by the flowing water.

● ● ●

The old man's truck had only one seat in front, so Carl rode in back on the open bed with Sachi and Seiku, bouncing down a narrow, muddy lane through the hills. He glanced at Sachi, whose hair blew around her face. She smiled at him. Seiku grinned into the wind.

Colors had never looked so vivid to Carl. Fragrances had never been so distinct. The storm had purged all drabness from the world.

When the truck turned onto the highway, Carl realized they weren't far from the camp. Before long he saw Flora's car, still in the ditch. "That's where we wrecked," he told Sachi.

She nodded.

They turned up the lane to the camp. It looked deserted. Carl climbed down and looked around. All the gear was there. He shouted but received no answer. Wind rippled the tent cloth, a forlorn sound. "Maybe they're at the village," he said.

They headed back out to the road and down to the village. The beach there was white as ground mirrors, the choppy sea astonishingly blue. The truck turned onto the gravel parking lot and stopped in front of the store.

At that moment, to Carl's unutterable relief, Rick hobbled out of the store, followed by Flora and Sharon. He remembered his dream and felt the warm net of safety his friends had cast around him.

"Carl!" Rick shouted as Carl climbed off the truck.

Flora dashed past Rick and grabbed Carl. "What happened?"

"Nothing too serious," Carl said, grinning.

"We didn't know what happened to you, buddy," Rick said. "We hoped we'd find you down here."

Flora began to cry. "I was so afraid." Sharon clung to her mother, snuffling.

"Shh, I'm all right," Carl said. "I went down to the beach last night and saw a light out in the water. This woman and her little boy were stranded on a rock in the storm. I swam out and helped them get to shore."

Sachi stepped forward to greet the others. "He saved us," she said. "You are Mrs. Connolly?"

Carl quickly made introductions. Rick and the old man shook hands.

Carl turned to Rick. "How are you?"

"Better."

"Did you ever find a mechanic?"

"He's due any minute," Rick replied.

"We wait here," Sachi said.

"No, that's not necessary," Carl said. "Please. You have work to do. When our car is fixed, we will come to your house."

"Okay. Come, Seiku." The three Okinawans climbed back onto the truck, and the old man drove them away.

As the sound of the engine faded, Carl had the feeling that they had been ghosts, angels, creatures of a dream. "How long have you been here?" he asked.

"Not long," Flora answered. "We looked everywhere for you and finally decided to try here. Carl, how are you hurt?" She touched the bandages lightly.

"Minor cuts. Look, why don't we get a pineapple drink?"

"Sounds good," Rick said.

Sharon tugged her mother's arm. "Mommy, why is Uncle Carl wearing a dress?"

Flora laughed. "I guess he lost his pants, honey. Carl, you do look funny in that skirt. What happened to your pants, anyway?"

He grinned. "They were ripped pretty bad, and Uza-san put this on me, I guess. Hey, it was a rough night."

"Well, we want to hear all about it."

They walked into the store, and Carl selected four brown bottles from the cooler. The man behind the counter opened the bottles, his hands smearing the beads of condensation on the brown glass. He handed Sharon the first bottle. She sniffed, put it tentatively to her lips, and sipped. "Yum!"

Rick paid and they all walked out. They settled themselves at a table in front of the store.

"Man, it's beautiful today," Carl said.

"You feel all right, really?" Rick said. "What about those bandages?"

"Cut myself on the rocks. Nothing, really." He reached down and realized he no longer had his knife. He tensed for a moment, then relaxed. Tipping up the bottle, he took a long swallow.

After a moment he set the bottle down with a resolute thump. "You know," he said. "I've been thinking. I think I really would like to stay here."

"Oh, Carl, come on," Flora said.

"I don't mean right now. I mean, go back south with you, then call my editors and see if they're interested in a series of articles. I don't know, maybe a book. I think I could do something good up here, a book on village life."

"Sounds interesting," Rick said.

"Sounds unrealistic to me," Flora said. "How would you live?"

"I have some money in savings at home. I could have some wired to me. And like I said, maybe a publisher would be interested and would give me an advance."

"But where would you stay?"

"That old man." He nodded. "I believe I could stay with them. They would let me, I'm sure."

"What's the woman's name? Sachi?" Flora asked.

"Yes," Carl said. "She had a husband too. But she lost him—last night."

"What?"

"I didn't tell you yet. Their boat crashed on the rocks. The husband was killed. I saw their light and swam out and found Sachi and her son perched on a rock. We grabbed a board and swam back."

"That's incredible," Rick said.

"Oh, Carl, I am so sorry."

"The poor boy doesn't even realize his father's dead."

Flora turned away. Rick put an arm around her shoulders.

Sharon looked up from her bottle. "What's the matter, Mommy?" she asked.

Flora turned to Carl. "I want to see that woman again, talk to her."

"We will. It's easy to get to their house. They live down a lane not far past the turnoff to the camp. I never even noticed it coming up."

"That's so sad about her husband," Flora said.

"They're searching for his body now."

"Can we help?" Rick said.

"Let's get the car fixed first. Then we'll see what we can do," Carl replied.

They heard a car approaching. "I think that's our mechanic now," Flora said.

The car, a muddy white Nissan, appeared on the road and turned into the parking area. It stopped several yards away.

Something stirred inside Carl. He stood up.

The car door opened. A man emerged, first one leg, then the other. He stood. That was when Carl saw the sling covering the man's left arm.

This was no mechanic.

Carl's eyes darted over the wide parking lot. No hope of escape there. He looked over his shoulder at the store—shelter or trap? He at least had to be sure his friends wouldn't be hurt.

Carl lunged toward the building. Then, seeing there was no hope of making it, he turned to face the man, who had scrambled toward him, drawing a pistol. He aimed it at Carl's body.

Flora screamed.

The gunman shot, once. Carl shouted as the bullet tore through him.

Rick jumped up, but the gunman seemed ready for him. He swiveled and fired.

But Rick jumped too far too fast. The shot went wild, the bullet thudding into the corner of the store building.

Rick's right foot slammed into the man's upper thigh, crumpling him as though his entire pelvic structure had been crushed. The man twisted, dropping first to the ground with a groan.

Flora and Sharon sat frozen.

Rick knelt to grab the gun hand, but the man wrenched it away with a snarl. Wheeling swiftly, Rick cocked his right arm and delivered a full-force karate chop to the back of his opponent's neck as he struggled to rise.

The man collapsed with a deep, final sigh, his cheek flat against the dirt. A trickle of blood slid from the corner of his mouth.

When Flora saw the man lying still, Rick standing over him, she ran to Carl.

"Carl!" she cried out. She knelt beside him, unsure where to put her hands.

His eyes were closed. His grimace had relaxed almost into a smile.

Flora touched his face, his hands. "Carl!" She bowed her head over his body, crying.

Sharon ran to her mother and clutched at her waist.

Rick came up from behind her and with strong, gentle

arms pulled Flora away. He knelt beside the body, feeling for a pulse.

The storekeeper, who had been crouching in his building, burst through the screen door. He waved his arms and shouted in Japanese.

Rick pulled away the bloody bandage, revealing a messy, gelatinous mass in the left ribcage. He gestured to the storekeeper.

"He's still alive," Rick said tersely in Japanese. "Get him into that car. Now."

The storekeeper barked out instructions to the villagers who now surrounded them. One man ran to the Nissan, its door still open, and started the engine. Several men lifted Carl gingerly and carried him to the car.

"Easy," Rick cautioned.

Flora could not speak. She had seen the blood, the wound. How could Carl survive that?

"Is he going to be all right, Mommy?" Sharon said, clinging to her arm.

Flora knelt down and hugged her daughter tightly, rocking her back and forth. "I don't know, honey."

"Hey, wait a minute!" Rick shouted.

The villagers had put Carl into the back seat and slammed the doors behind him. The car took off in a spray of gravel.

A man approached them. From the gray at his temples and his stern but relaxed manner they pegged him as someone with authority. The sleeves of his well-worn white shirt were rolled up over brown forearms; he wore weathered gray trousers and sandals.

"There is a clinic at Hedo," he said in good English. "Do you have a car?"

"It's broken down," Rick said. "We've got to follow that car. Our friend . . ."

"No problem," he said. "Come, we will follow them in my son's truck."

They piled into an ancient three-wheel pickup truck and bounced down the road to the north, following the car that carried their friend—and praying fiercely for his life.

CHAPTER 24

• • •

Malicious elves danced a tattoo on Carl's chest. They stared down at his face with cunning cruelty, aiming covert kicks into his ribs. He wanted to reach for them, grab them, and wring their necks, but his arms lay limp.

Carl opened his eyes and realized he was underwater, like a sea urchin in the shallows watching the topside world through a silvery film. Three faces swirled into and out of focus. They looked dimly familiar, inhabitants of a peaceful planet he had once visited. The aroma of tea and fish seemed to surround them. The sun set and the world darkened.

Three faces appeared again, different this time. One towered over the others, a brown lion—the cowardly lion in *The Wizard of Oz*? No, this one exuded courage. The second face, at middle height, was a pale moon haloed by glossy black, and the third was the same in miniature. They disappeared.

Later, in a vivid dream, Carl observed his own funeral. He watched from a pulpit pew as he waited to deliver his own eulogy. A small crowd, most of them unknown to him, sat quietly except for an occasional cough, whisper, or a child's voice suppressed by a parent. Flora, dressed in crisp black, followed by Sharon and Rick, walked down the aisle to a pew evidently reserved for close friends. The air weighed heavily with the smell of flowers drifting on a breeze of organ music.

Flora dabbed her eyes with a handkerchief. Beside her Sharon fidgeted. On her other side Rick sat erect, obviously uncomfortable in a restrictive suit.

Carl looked past them to see Sachi, Seiku, and Uzasan make their way with nervous modesty down the aisle. Turning, Flora motioned to them as though expecting them. She rose and leaned past Rick to hug Sachi. Then Flora, Rick, and Sharon moved down to allow room in the pew. Seiku's bewildered eyes revealed his realization, finally, of his own father's death. Nevertheless, he craned forward to look over at Sharon curiously.

They sat back as the organ music faded. Carl stood up, clearing his throat, and approached the podium with his Bible. The audience showed no surprise at his presence. He had his speech rehearsed, taken from the book of Daniel about the ordeal in the fiery furnace when God kept the flames from devouring the faithful. Carl empathized with the plight of Daniel's three compatriots, Shadrach, Meshach, and Abednego. They were prepared to take the straight path into death.

He could not find the passage he was seeking, for the Bible seemed locked open to a particular passage, one verse underlined in red. Anger and confusion flooded Carl. The other pages seemed stuck together. This was getting embarrassing. Reluctantly, he forced himself to read the marked Scripture: "My command is this: Love each other as I have loved you. Greater love has no one than this, that he lay down his life for his friends."

Carl remembered Sachi, Seiku, and the night on the rock. Sachi's husband had died for his family. And Carl—he had thought he was leaping into death, but instead he had plunged into life—a different kind of life. He had been a man out of sync, unbalanced, his life all in tatters. In this new life everything had changed.

He suddenly realized the church was filled with applause. He looked up in astonishment, wondering whether he had read the verse aloud, and saw the auditorium packed with everyone he had ever known and loved. All standing, they were clapping vigorously, eyes radiant.

Carl wept.

●　●　●

Carl lay awake in his hospital bed in Naha, relishing the morning light that came in his windows. As his eyes followed the play of light through the curtains, his mind focused on a single memory, more powerful than all his childhood hauntings: the memory of that white-hot explosion of adrenaline, his spirit-shout into which all his life and power had been channeled, and the simultaneous impact of the bullet in his ribs. It had struck him like a baseball hit by a pro slugger.

After that, darkness. Jumbled dreams, some peaceful, some hellish.

Morning shone so cleanly on him now. It struck him that he had not expected it, this new day.

A murmur sounded outside his room, followed by a tap at the door.

"Come in." His voice was weak.

Flora's face peeked in, followed by Rick's. They approached Carl's bedside.

"Can I hug you?" Flora said.

"Better not." But he took her hand, and Rick squeezed his arm.

"How are you feeling, buddy?" said the big man.

Carl nodded. "Fine." The frailness of his voice irritated him. How could he tell them that inside, beyond the injuries to his body, life surged through him? Maybe they could see it in his eyes.

"Does it hurt very much?" Flora asked.

"Only when I breathe." He smiled.

"I'll bet they have you doped up too," Rick said.

Carl realized he must be right. He felt woozy and ethereal. But at least he was conscious.

"Can you remember anything?" Flora asked.

Carl looked at the wall in front of him. "The shot. I can remember the shot."

"Then you do remember," Rick said. "I'd wondered."

"Anything after that?" Flora asked.

He shook his head. "Only dreams."

"The doctor said you must have hit your head when you fell," Rick told him. "It must have knocked you out. The bullet busted up your ribs and punctured a lung."

"Missed your heart, thank God," Flora added.

Carl turned his face back to them, warmed by their presence. "What happened to him?" he asked them.

Flora smiled grimly. "Rick took care of him—for good."

Carl looked at his friend, perceiving instantly what Flora had missed—the immense guilt Rick must feel for taking another man's life. "I'm sorry," Carl said softly.

Rick returned his gaze without speaking and slowly nodded.

"If Rick hadn't broken the man's arm earlier he probably wouldn't have missed your heart, Carl," Flora informed him. "He had to shoot one-handed. The police said that's the only thing that saved you, most likely. That and Rick here."

"Police, huh?" Carl said.

"Oh yes, we've had to give statements," Flora answered. "You will too, eventually. They know all about it now, even got in touch with your editors. They confirmed the whole thing. Your newspaper wants to hear from you as soon as you're able, by the way."

Carl remembered another dream he had had, one of the peaceful ones. His editors seemed connected with it somehow.

"We can't stay long," Rick said. "We're only supposed to stay ten minutes. You need to rest."

Carl nodded but did not let go of Flora's hand.

"Did you know your friend Sachi and her little boy and father came to see you?" Flora asked.

Carl shook his head, vaguely recalling faces.

"Drove all the way from their village," she went on. "That's a long way. I said I'd write them when you got better. They want to see you."

He closed his eyes. He remembered the dream now: that clearing where Sachi, Seiku, and Uza-san lived. He saw himself there, sitting beside the stream, writing in a notebook—writing articles for his newspaper, perhaps? He smiled at the memory of the dream and opened his eyes to look at his friends, but they had slipped out quietly, thinking he had fallen asleep.

● ● ●

Cerulean. Azure. How about just plain blue? Actually, Carl decided, no word could do justice to that cirrus-grazed sky so bright and pure above the green northern hills of the island.

As the bus rumbled away down the lonely road, Carl hoisted his duffel bag—gingerly, for his side still ached—and set off up the lane that led into the hills.

A Pacific breeze gusted at his back. The afternoon sun cast tree shadows across the lane, and the woods divulged their secrets of bird song and flower scent.

Carl stopped to rest. No need to hurry. His ribs and lung had mended, leaving an ugly brown scar, but a dim soreness lived in his side. He would get over it. He would bathe it in cold stream water.

He continued. A gang of seagulls circled overhead, hurling epithets his way.

"Same to you!" he said and grinned.

At last he topped a slight rise and saw the clearing

where two houses and a shed stood amid a sprawl of gardens. No one was in sight.

Carl set his duffel bag down in the yard. Among other things the bag contained a tent so he would not have to impose on anyone.

"Anybody home?" he called.

He walked down the path toward the stream. Down below he saw Sachi kneeling by the water washing clothes.

"Hello!" he called as he approached.

She turned, her face wearing a distracted frown. Seeing him, she smiled, raising a soapy hand to brush a strand of hair from her face.

He took a deep breath, then went forward to meet her.

Also by Ernest Herndon

Morning Morning True: A Novel of New Guinea

In this fast-paced novel, hot-shot missionary Powers Stivell, a twenty-four-year-old jungle veteran, leads an expedition into the remote mountains of Papua New Guinea. From the outset, delays and setbacks plague the group, their guide Yalu, and a handful of carriers and assistants. But when the safari reaches its objective, the village of Engati, the trouble truly begins. After an enthusiastic reception by their tribal hosts, Powers is frustrated in his attempt to preach. Then Yalu refuses to translate his message into the native tongue and blocks their planned departure.

Finally the hauntingly evil Yalu becomes unstoppable—and deadly. What ensues is a roller-coaster ride of peril and emotion, told realistically by an author who himself has experienced rugged journeys in the New Guinea interior.

About the Author

Ernest Herndon has traveled extensively throughout North and Central America, the Far East, and the South Pacific. A reporter for the McComb, Mississippi, *Enterprise-Journal* newspaper, he enjoys backpacking, camping, canoeing, karate, and guitar. He lives in rural southwest Mississippi with his wife, Angelyn, son, Andy, five dogs, and five cats.